Grimm's

Fairy Tales

GRIMM'S
FAIRY TALES

Illustrated by Jiří Trnka

HAMLYN

London • New York • Sydney • Toronto

First published 1961
Revised edition 1968
Fourth Impression (Revised) 1973

Designed and produced by ARTIA

Published by THE HAMLYN PUBLISHING GROUP LIMITED
London ● New York ● Sydney ● Toronto
Hamlyn House, Feltham, Middlesex, England

ISBN 0 601 07323 1

CONTENTS

BRIAR ROSE

A long time ago there lived a King and Queen, who said every day, 'If only we had a child!' but for a long time they had none.

And then one day, as the Queen was bathing, a frog crept out of the water on to the land, and said to her: 'Your wish shall be fulfilled; before a year has passed you shall bring a daughter into the world.'

The frog's words came true. The Queen had a little girl who was so beautiful that the King could not contain himself for joy, and prepared a great feast. He invited not only his relations, friends and acquaintances, but the fairies, in order that they might be favourably and kindly disposed towards the child. There were thirteen of them in the kingdom, but as the King had only twelve golden plates for them to eat from, one of the fairies had to stay at home.

The feast was held with all splendour, and when it came to an end the fairies all presented the child with a magic gift. One gave her virtue, another beauty, a third riches, and so on, with everything in the world that she could wish for.

When eleven of the fairies had said their say, the thirteenth suddenly appeared. She wanted to revenge herself for not having been invited. Without greeting anyone, or even glancing at the company, she called out in a loud voice: 'The Princess shall prick herself with a distaff in her fifteenth year and shall fall down dead.' And without another word she turned and left the hall.

Everyone was terror-struck; but the twelfth fairy, whose wish was still un-spoken, stepped forward. She could not cancel the curse, but could only soften it, so she said: 'It shall not be death, but a deep sleep lasting a hundred years, into which your daughter shall fall.'

The King was so anxious to guard his dear child from the misfortune that he sent out a command that all the distaffs in the whole kingdom should be burned.

As time went on all the promises of the fairies came true. The Princess grew up to be so beautiful, modest, kind and clever that everyone who saw her could not but love her. Now it happened that on the very day when she was fifteen years old the King and Queen were away from home, and the Princess was left quite alone in the castle. She wandered about over the entire place, looking at rooms and halls as she pleased, and at last she came to an old tower. She ascended a narrow, winding staircase and reached a little door. A rusty key was sticking in the lock, and when she turned it, the door flew open. In a little room sat an old woman with a spindle, spinning her flax busily.

'Good day, Granny,' said the Princess, 'what are you doing?'

'I am spinning,' said the old woman, and nodded her head.

'What is the thing that whirls round so merrily?' asked the Princess; and she took the spindle and tried to spin too.

But she had scarcely touched it before the curse was fulfilled, and she pricked her finger with the spindle. The instant she felt the prick she fell upon the bed which was standing near, and lay still in a deep sleep which spread over the whole castle.

The King and Queen, who had just come home and had stepped into the hall, went to sleep, and all their courtiers with them. The horses went to sleep in the stable, the dogs in the yard, the doves on the roof, the flies on the wall; yes, even the fire flickering on the hearth grew still and went to sleep, and the roast meat stopped crackling. The cook, who was pulling the scullion's hair because he had made some mistake, let him go and went to sleep. The wind dropped, and on the trees in front of the castle not a leaf stirred.

Round the castle a hedge of briar roses began to grow up; every year it grew higher, till at last it surrounded the whole castle so that nothing could be seen of it, not even the flags on the roof.

But there was a legend in the land about the lovely sleeping Briar Rose, as the King's daughter was called, and from time to time princes came and tried to force a way through the hedge into the castle. They found it impossible, for the thorns, as though they had hands, held them fast, and the princes remained caught in them without being able to free themselves, and so died a miserable death.

After many, many years a Prince came again to the country and heard an old man tell of the castle which stood behind the briar hedge, in which a most beautiful maiden called Briar Rose had been asleep for the last hundred years, and with her slept the King, Queen, and all the courtiers. He knew also, from his grandfather, that many princes had already come and sought to pierce through the briar hedge, and had remained caught in it and died a sad death.

Then the young Prince said, 'I am not afraid; I am determined to go and look upon the lovely Briar Rose.'

The good old man did all in his power to dissuade him, but the Prince would not listen to his words.

Now, however, the hundred years were just ended, and the day had come when Briar Rose was to wake up again. When the Prince approached the briar hedge it was in blossom, and was covered with beautiful large flowers, which made way for him of their own accord and let him pass unharmed, and then closed up again into a hedge behind him.

In the courtyard he saw the horses and brindled hounds lying asleep; on the roof sat the doves with their heads under their wings. And when he went into the house the flies were asleep on the walls, and near the throne lay the King

8

and Queen. In the kitchen was the cook, with his hand raised as though about to strike the scullion, and the maid sat with the black fowl in her lap which she was about to pluck.

He went on further, and all was so still that he could hear his own breathing. At last he reached the tower, and opened the door into the little room where Briar Rose was asleep. There she lay, looking so beautiful that he could not take his eyes off her; he bent down and gave her a kiss. As he touched her, Briar Rose opened her eyes and looked lovingly at him.

Then they went down together; and the King woke up, and the Queen, and all the courtiers, and looked at each other with astonished eyes. The horses in the stable stood up and shook themselves, the hounds leaped about and wagged their tails and the doves on the roof lifted their heads from under their wings, looked round, and flew into the fields. The flies on the walls began to crawl again, the fire in the kitchen roused itself and blazed up and cooked the food, the meat began to crackle, and the cook boxed the scullion's ears so soundly that he screamed aloud, while the maid finished plucking the fowl. Then the wedding of the Prince and Briar Rose was celebrated with all splendour, and they lived happily till the end of their days.

LITTLE RED RIDING-HOOD

Once upon a time there was a dear little girl who was loved by everyone who looked at her, but most of all by her grandmother, and there was nothing she would not have given to the child. Once she gave her a little hood of red velvet, which suited her so well that she would never wear anything else; so she was always called 'Little Red Riding-Hood'.

One day her mother said to her, 'Come, Little Red Riding-Hood, here is a piece of cake and a bottle of wine. Take them to your grandmother; she is ill and weak, and they will do her good. Set out before it gets hot, and when you are going, walk nicely and quietly and do not run off the path, or you may fall and break the bottle, and then your grandmother will get nothing; and when you go into her room, don't forget to say "Good-morning", and don't peep into every corner before you do it.'

'I will take great care,' said Little Red Riding-Hood to her mother, and gave her hand on it.

The grandmother lived out in the wood, half a league from the village, and just as Little Red Riding-Hood entered the wood, a wolf met her. Little Red Riding-Hood did not know what a wicked creature he was, and was not at all afraid of him.

'Good-day, Little Red Riding-Hood,' said he.

'Thank you kindly, wolf.'

'Whither away so early, Little Red Riding-Hood?'

'To my grandmother's.'

'What have you got in your apron?'

'Cake and wine; yesterday was baking-day, so poor sick grandmother is to have something good, to make her stronger.'

'Where does your grandmother live, Little Red Riding-Hood?'

'A good quarter of a league farther on in the wood; her house stands under the three large oak-trees; the nut-trees are just below. You surely must know it,' replied Little Red Riding-Hood.

The wolf thought to himself, 'What a tender young creature! What a nice plump mouthful! She will be better to eat than the old woman. I must act craftily, so as to catch both.' So he walked for a short time by the side of Little Red Riding-Hood, and then he said, 'See, Little Red Riding-Hood, how pretty the flowers are about here—why do you not look round? I believe, too, that you do not hear how sweetly the little birds are singing; you walk gravely along as if you were going to school, while everything else out here in the wood is merry.'

Little Red Riding-Hood raised her eyes, and when she saw the sunbeams dancing here and there through the trees, and pretty flowers growing everywhere, she thought, 'Suppose I take grandmother a fresh nosegay; that would please her too. It is so early in the day that I shall still get there in good time.' And so she ran from the path into the wood to look for flowers. And whenever she had picked one, she fancied that she saw a still prettier one farther on, and ran after it, and so got deeper and deeper into the wood.

Meanwhile, the wolf ran straight to the grandmother's house and knocked at the door.

'Who is there?'

'Little Red Riding-Hood,' replied the wolf. 'She is bringing cake and wine; open the door.'

'Lift the latch,' called out the grandmother. 'I am too weak, and cannot get up.'

The wolf lifted the latch, the door flew open, and without saying a word he went straight to the grandmother's bed and devoured her. Then he put on her clothes, dressed himself in her cap, laid himself in bed and drew the curtains.

Little Red Riding-Hood, however, had been running about picking flowers, and when she had gathered so many that she could carry no more, she remembered her grandmother, and set out on the way to her.

She was surprised to find the cottage door standing open, and when she went into the room, she had such a strange feeling that she said to herself, 'Oh dear! how uneasy I feel today, and at other times I like being with grandmother so much.' She called out 'Good-morning', but received no answer; so she went to the bed and drew back the curtains. There lay her grandmother with her cap pulled far over her face, and looking very strange.

'Oh! grandmother,' she said, 'what big ears you have!'

'The better to hear you with, my child,' was the reply.

'But, grandmother, what big eyes you have!' she said.

'The better to see you with, my dear.'

'But, grandmother, what large hands you have!'

'The better to hug you with.'

'Oh! but, grandmother, what a terrible big mouth you have!'

'The better to eat you with.'

And scarcely had the wolf said this, than with one bound he was out of bed and had swallowed up Red Riding-Hood.

When the wolf had appeased his appetite, he lay down again in the bed, fell asleep and began to snore very loud. The huntsman was just passing the house, and thought to himself, 'How the old woman is snoring! I must just see if she wants anything.' So he went into the room, and when he came to the bed he saw that the wolf was lying in it. 'Do I find you here, you old sinner!' said he. 'I have long sought you!' Then just as he was going to fire at him, it occurred to him that the wolf might have devoured the grandmother and that she might still be saved, so he did not fire, but took a pair of scissors and began to cut open the stomach of the sleeping wolf.

When he had made two snips, he saw the little red hood shining, and then he made two snips more, and the little girl sprang out, crying, 'Ah, how frightened I have been! How dark it was inside the wolf!' And after that the aged grandmother came out alive also, but scarcely able to breathe. Little Red Riding-Hood, however, quickly fetched great stones with which they filled the wolf's body, and when he awoke, he wanted to run away, but the stones were so heavy that he fell down at once, and fell dead.

Then all three were delighted. The huntsman drew off the wolf's skin and went home with it; the grandmother ate the cake and drank the wine which Red Riding-Hood had brought, and revived, but Red Riding-Hood thought to herself, 'As long as I live, I will never leave the path by myself, to run into the wood, when my mother has forbidden me to do so.'

It is also related that once when Little Red Riding-Hood was again taking cakes to the old grandmother, another wolf spoke to her and tried to entice her from the path. Red Riding-Hood was, however, on her guard, and went straight forward on her way, and told her grandmother that she had met the wolf, and that he had said 'good-morning' to her, but with such a wicked look in his eyes that if they had not been on the public road she was certain he would have eaten her up. 'Well,' said the grandmother, 'we will shut the door, that he may not come in.'

Soon afterwards, the wolf knocked, and cried, 'Open the door, grandmother, I am Little Red Riding-Hood, and am fetching you some cakes.' But they did not speak or open the door, so the grey-beard stole twice or thrice round the house, and at last jumped on the roof, intending to wait until Red Riding-Hood went home in the evening and then to steal after her and devour her in the darkness.

But the grandmother saw what was in his thoughts. In front of the house was a great stone trough, so she said to the child, 'Take a pail, Red Riding-Hood; I made some sausages yesterday, so carry the water in which I boiled them to the trough.'

Red Riding-Hood carried until the great trough was quite full. Then the smell of the sausages reached the wolf, and he sniffed and peeped down, and at last stretched out his neck so far that he could no longer keep his footing and began to slip, and slipped down from the roof straight into the great trough, and was drowned.

But Red Riding-Hood went joyously home, and from that time was safe from harm.

CINDERELLA

The wife of a rich man fell sick, and as she felt that her end was drawing near she called her only daughter to her bedside and said, 'Dear child, be good and pious, and then the good God will always protect you, and I will look down on you from heaven and be near you.' Thereupon she closed her eyes and departed.

Every day the girl went out to her mother's grave and wept, and she remained pious and good. When winter came the snow spread a white sheet over the grave, and when the spring sun had drawn it off again, the man had taken another wife.

The woman had brought two daughters into the house with her, who were beautiful and fair of face, but vile and black of heart. Now a bad time began for the poor stepchild. 'Is the stupid goose to sit in the parlour with us?' they said. 'He who wants to eat bread must earn it; out with the kitchen-wench.' They took her pretty clothes away from her, put an old grey bed-gown on her, and gave her wooden shoes. 'Just look at the proud princess, how decked out she is!' they cried, and laughed, and led her into the kitchen.

There she had to do hard work from morning till night: get up before daybreak, carry water, light fires, cook and wash. Besides this, the sisters did her every imaginable injury—they mocked her, and emptied her peas and lentils into the ashes, so that she was forced to sit and pick them out again. In the evening, when she had worked till she was weary, she had no bed to go to, but had to sleep by the fireside in the ashes. And as on that account she always looked dusty and dirty, they called her Cinderella.

It happened that the father was going to the fair, and he asked his two step-daughters what he should bring back for them. 'Beautiful dresses,' said one; 'Pearls and jewels,' said the second.

'And you, Cinderella, what would you like?'

'Father, break off for me the first branch which knocks against your hat on the way home.'

So he bought beautiful dresses, pearls and jewels for his two stepdaughters, and on his way home, as he was riding through a green thicket, a hazel twig brushed against him and knocked off his hat. Then he broke off the branch and took it with him.

When he reached home he gave his stepdaughters the things which they had wished for, and to Cinderella he gave the branch from the hazel-bush. Cinderella thanked him, went to her mother's grave and planted the branch on it, and wept so much that the tears fell down on it and watered it. It grew, and became a hand-

15

some tree. Three times a day Cinderella went and sat beneath it, and wept and prayed, and a little white bird always came on the tree; and if Cinderella expressed a wish, the bird threw down to her what she had wished for.

It happened, however, that the King ordered a festival which was to last three days, and to which all the beautiful young girls in the country were invited, in order that his son might choose himself a bride. When the two stepsisters heard that they, too, were to appear among the number, they were delighted, called Cinderella, and said, 'Comb our hair for us, brush our shoes and fasten our buckles, for we are going to the festival at the King's palace.'

Cinderella obeyed, but wept, because she too would have liked to go with them to the dance; and she begged her stepmother to allow her to do so. 'You go, Cinderella!' said she; 'dusty and dirty as you are, you would go to the festival? You do not have clothes and shoes, and yet you would dance?' As, however, Cinderella went on asking, the stepmother at last said, 'I have emptied a dish of lentils into the ashes for you; if you have picked them out again in two hours, you shall go with us.'

The girl went through the back door into the garden, and called, 'You tame pigeons, you turtle-doves, and all you birds beneath the sky, come and help me to put

> The good into the pot,
> The bad into the crop.'

Then two white pigeons came in by the kitchen window, and afterwards the turtle-doves, and at last all the birds beneath the sky, came whirring and crowding in, and alighted amongst the ashes. And the pigeons nodded with their heads and began to pick, pick, pick, pick, and the rest began also to pick, pick, pick, pick, and gathered all the good grains into the dish. Hardly had one hour passed before they were finished, and all flew out again. Then the girl took the dish to her stepmother, and was glad, and believed that now she would be allowed to go with them to the festival. But the stepmother said, 'No, Cinderella, you have no clothes and you cannot dance; you would only be laughed at.' And as Cinderella wept at this, the stepmother said, 'If you can pick two dishes of lentils out of the ashes for me in one hour, you shall go with us.' And she thought to herself, 'That she most certainly cannot do.'

When the stepmother had emptied the two dishes of lentils amongst the ashes, the girl went through the back door into the garden and cried, 'You tame pigeons, you turtle-doves, and all you birds under heaven, come and help me to put

> The good into the pot,
> The bad into the crop.'

Then two white pigeons came in by the kitchen window, and afterwards the turtle-doves, and at length all the birds beneath the sky, came whirring and crowding in, and alighted amongst the ashes. And the doves nodded with their heads and began to pick, pick, pick, pick, and the others began also to pick, pick, pick, pick, and gathered all the good seeds into the dishes, and before half an hour was over they had already finished, and all flew out again. Then the girl carried the dishes to the stepmother and was delighted, and believed that she might now go with them to the festival. But the stepmother said, 'All this will not help you; you shall not go with us, for you have no clothes and cannot dance; we should be ashamed of you!' With this she turned her back on Cinderella, and hurried away with her two proud daughters.

As no one was now at home, Cinderella went to her mother's grave beneath the hazel-tree, and cried:

'Shiver and quiver, my little tree,
Silver and gold throw down over me.'

Then the bird threw a gold-and-silver dress down to her, and slippers embroidered with silk and silver. She put on the dress with all speed, and went to the festival. Her stepsisters and the stepmother, however, did not know her, and thought she must be a foreign princess, for she looked so beautiful in the gleaming dress. They never once thought of Cinderella, and believed that she was sitting at home in the dirt, picking lentils out of the ashes. The Prince went to meet her, took her by the hand and danced with her. He would dance with no other maiden, and never let go of her hand, and if anyone else came to invite her, he said, 'This is *my* partner.'

She danced till it was evening, and then she wanted to go home. But the King's son said, 'I will go with you and bear you company,' for he wished to see to whom the beautiful girl belonged. She escaped from him, however, and sprang into the pigeon-house. The King's son waited until her father came, and then he told him that the strange maiden had leapt into the pigeon-house. The old man thought 'Can it be Cinderella?' and they had to bring him an axe and a pickaxe so that he might hew the pigeon-house to pieces, but no one was inside it.

And when they got home, Cinderella lay in her dirty clothes among the ashes, and a dim little oil-lamp was burning on the mantelpiece, for Cinderella had jumped quickly down from the back of the pigeon-house and had run to the little hazel-tree, and there she had taken off her beautiful clothes and laid them down, and the bird had taken them away again, and then she had placed herself in the kitchen amongst the ashes in her grey gown.

Next day, when the festival began afresh and her parents and the stepsisters had gone once more, Cinderella went to the hazel-tree and said:

'Shiver and quiver, my little tree,
Silver and gold throw down over me.'

Then the bird threw down a much more beautiful dress than on the preceding day. And when Cinderella appeared at the festival in this dress, everyone was astonished at her beauty. The King's son had waited until she came, and instantly took her by the hand and danced with no one but her. When others came and invited her, he said, 'She is *my* partner.'

When evening came she wished to leave, and the King's son followed her and wished to see into which house she went. But she sprang away from him, and into the garden behind the house. There stood a beautiful tall tree on which hung the most magnificent pears. She clambered so nimbly between the branches, like a squirrel, that the King's son did not know where she was gone. He waited until her father came, and said to him, 'The strange maiden has escaped from me, and I believe she has climbed up the pear-tree.'

The father thought, 'Can it be Cinderella?' and had an axe brought and cut the tree down, but no one was on it.

And when they got into the kitchen, Cinderella lay there amongst the ashes, as usual, for she had jumped down on the other side of the tree, had taken the beautiful dress to the bird in the little hazel-tree, and put on her grey gown.

On the third day, when her parents and sisters had gone, Cinderella once more went to the little tree and said:

'Shiver and quiver, my little tree,
Silver and gold throw down over me.'

And now the bird threw down to her a dress which was more splendid and magnificent than any she had yet had, and the slippers were golden. And when she went to the festival in this dress, no one knew how to speak for astonishment. The King's son danced with her only, and if anyone invited her to dance, he said, 'She is *my* partner.'

When evening came, Cinderella wished to leave, and the King's son was anxious to go with her, but she escaped from him so quickly that he could not follow her. The King's son had, however, used a stratagem, and had caused the whole staircase to be smeared with pitch, and there, when she ran down, the girl's left slipper remained sticking. The King's son picked it up, and it was small and dainty, and all golden.

Next morning, he went with it to the father, and said to him, 'No one shall be my wife but she whose foot this golden slipper fits.'

Then the two sisters were glad, for they had pretty feet. The eldest went with

the shoe into her room and wanted to try it on, and her mother stood by. But she could not get her big toe into it, and the shoe was too small for her. Then her mother gave her a knife, and said, 'Cut the toe off; when you are Queen you will have no more need to go on foot.'

The girl cut the toe off, forced the foot into the shoe, swallowed the pain, and went out to the King's son. Then he took her on his horse as his bride and rode away with her. They were, however, obliged to pass the grave, and there, on the hazel-tree, sat the two pigeons and cried:

> 'Turn and peep, turn and peep,
> There's blood within the shoe,
> The shoe it is too small for her,
> The true bride waits for you.'

Then he looked at her foot and saw how the blood was flowing from it. He turned his horse round and took the false bride home again, and said she was not the true one, and that the other sister was to put the shoe on.

Then this one went into her chamber and got her toes safely into the shoe, but her heel was too large. So her mother gave her a knife, and said. 'Cut a bit off your heel; when you are Queen you will have no more need to go on foot.'

The maiden cut a bit off her heel, forced her foot into the shoe, swallowed the pain, and went out to the King's son. He took her on his horse as his bride and rode away with her, but when they passed by the hazel-tree, two little pigeons sat on it and cried,

> 'Turn and peep, turn and peep,
> There's blood within the shoe,
> The shoe it is too small for her,
> The true bride waits for you.'

Then he looked down at her foot and saw how the blood was running out of her shoe, and how it had stained her white stocking. Then he turned his horse and took the false bride home again. 'This also is not the right one,' said he, 'have you no other daughter?'

'No,' said the man, 'there is only a little stunted kitchen-wench which my late wife left behind her, but she cannot possibly be the bride.'

The King's son said he was to send her up to him; but the mother answered, 'Oh no, she is much too dirty; she cannot show herself!'

He absolutely insisted on it, and Cinderella had to be called. She first washed her hands and face clean, and then went and bowed down before the King's son, who gave her the golden shoe. Then she seated herself on a stool, drew her foot out of the heavy wooden shoe, and put it into the slipper, which fitted like a glove. And when she rose up and the King's son looked at her face, he recognised the beautiful maiden who had danced with him, and cried, 'That is the true bride!'

The stepmother and the two sisters were terrified and became pale with rage; the King's son, however, took Cinderella on his horse and rode away with her. As they passed by the hazel-tree, the two white doves cried,

'Turn and peep, turn and peep,
No blood is in the shoe,
The shoe is not too small for her,
The true bride rides with you.'

and when they had cried that, the two came flying down and placed themselves on Cinderella's shoulders, one on the right, the other on the left, and remained sitting there, until she reached the palace.

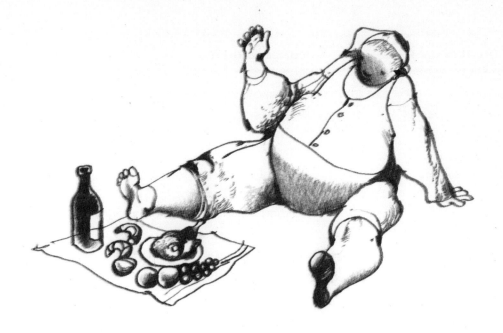

THE WISHING-TABLE, THE GOLD-ASS
AND THE CUDGEL IN THE SACK

There was once upon a time a tailor who had three sons, and only one goat. But as the goat supported the whole of them with her milk, she was obliged to have good food, and to be taken every day to pasture. The sons, therefore, did this in turn. Once the eldest took her to the churchyard, where the finest herbs were to be found, and let her eat and run about there. At night when it was time to go home he asked, 'Goat, have you had enough?' The goat answered,

'I have eaten so much,
Not a leaf more I'll touch, meh! meh!'

23

'Come home, then,' said the youth, and took hold of the cord round her neck, led her into the stable and tied her up securely.

'Well,' said the old tailor, 'has the goat had as much food as she ought?'

'Oh,' answered the son, 'she has eaten so much, not a leaf more she'll touch.'

But the father wished to satisfy himself, and went down to the stable, stroked the dear animal and asked, 'Goat, are you satisfied?' The goat answered,

'Wherewithal should I be satisfied?
Among the graves I leapt about,
And found no food, so went without, meh! meh!'

'What do I hear?' cried the tailor, and ran upstairs and said to the youth, 'Hollo, you liar; you said the goat had had enough, and have let her hunger!' and in his anger he took the yard-measure from the wall, and drove him out with blows.

Next day it was the turn of the second son, who looked out for a place in the fence of the garden, where nothing but good herbs grew, and the goat cleared them all off. At night when he wanted to go home, he asked, 'Goat, are you satisfied?' The goat answered,

'I have eaten so much,
Not a leaf more I'll touch, meh! meh!'

'Come home, then,' said the youth, and led her home and tied her up in the stable.

'Well,' said the old tailor, 'has the goat had as much food as she ought?'

'Oh,' answered the son, 'she has eaten so much, not a leaf more she'll touch.'

The tailor would not rely on this, but went down to the stable and said, 'Goat, have you had enough?' The goat answered,

'Wherewithal should I be satisfied?
Among the fences I leapt about,
And found no food, so went without, meh! meh!'

'The godless wretch!' cried the tailor, 'to let such a good animal hunger,' and he ran up and drove the youth out of doors with the yard-measure.

Now came the turn of the third son, who wanted to do the thing well, and sought out some bushes with the finest leaves, and let the goat devour them. In the evening, when he wanted to go home, he asked, 'Goat, have you had enough?' The goat answered,

'I have eaten so much,
Not a leaf more I'll touch, meh! meh!'

'Come home, then,' said the youth, and led her into the stable and tied her up. 'Well,' said the old tailor, 'has the goat had a proper amount of food?' 'She has eaten so much, not a leaf more she'll touch.'

The tailor did not trust to that, but went down and asked, 'Goat, have you had enough?' The wicked beast answered,

'Wherewithal should I be satisfied?
Among the fields I leapt about,
And found no leaves, so went without, meh! meh!'

'Oh, the brood of liars!' cried the tailor, 'each as wicked and forgetful of his duty as the other! You shall no longer make a fool of me,' and, quite beside himself with anger, he ran upstairs and belaboured the poor young fellow so vigorously with the yard-measure that he sprang out of the house.

The old tailor was now alone with his goat. Next morning he went down into the stable, caressed the goat, and said, 'Come, my dear little animal, I will take you to feed myself.' He took her by the rope and conducted her to green hedges, and amongst milfoil, and whatever else goats like to eat. 'There you may for once eat to your heart's content,' said he to her, and let her browse till evening. When he asked, 'Goat, are you satisfied?' she replied,

'I have eaten so much,
Not a leaf more I'll touch, meh! meh!'

'Come home, then,' said the tailor, and led her into the stable and tied her fast. When he was going away, he turned round again and said, 'Well, are you satisfied for once?' But the goat did not behave better to him, and cried,

'Wherewithal should I be satisfied?
Among the fields I leapt about,
And found no leaves, so went without, meh! meh!'

When the tailor heard that, he was shocked, and saw clearly that he had driven away his three sons without cause. 'Wait, you ungrateful creature,' cried he, 'it is not enough to drive you forth, I will mark you so that you will no more dare to show yourself amongst honest tailors.' In great haste he ran upstairs, fetched his razor, lathered the goat's head, and shaved her as clean as the palm of his hand. And as the yard-measure would have been too good for her, he brought the horse-whip, and gave her such cuts with it that she ran away in violent haste.

When the tailor was thus left quite alone in his house he fell into great grief, and would gladly have had his sons back again, but no one knew whither they were gone.

The eldest had apprenticed himself to a joiner, and learnt industriously and indefatigably, and when the time came for him to go travelling his master presented him with a little table which had no particular appearance, and was made of common wood, but it had one good property; if anyone set it out, and said, 'Little table, spread thyself,' the good little table was at once covered with a clean little cloth, and a plate was there, and a knife and fork beside it, and dishes with boiled meats and roasted meats, as many as there was room for, and a great glass of red wine shone so that it made the heart glad. The young journeyman thought, 'With this thou hast enough for thy whole life,' and went joyously about the world and never troubled himself at all whether an inn was good or bad, or if anything was to be found in it or not. When it suited him he did not enter an inn at all, but in the plain, in a wood, a meadow, or wherever he fancied, he took his little table off his back, set it down before him, and said, 'Spread thyself,' and then everything appeared that his heart desired.

At length he took it into his head to go back to his father, whose anger would now be appeased, and who would willingly receive him with his wishing-table. It came to pass that, on his way home, he came one evening to an inn which was filled with guests. They bade him welcome, and invited him to sit and eat with them, for otherwise he would have difficulty in getting anything. 'No,' answered the joiner, 'I will not take the few bites out of your mouths; rather than that, you shall be my guests.'

They laughed, and thought he was jesting with them; he, however, placed his wooden table in the middle of the room, and said, 'Little table, spread thyself.' Instantly it was covered with food, so good that the host could never have procured it, and the smell of it ascended pleasantly to the nostrils of the guests. 'Fall to, dear friends,' said the joiner, and the guests, when they saw that he meant it, did not need to be asked twice, but drew near, pulled out their knives and attacked it valiantly. And what surprised them the most was that when a dish became empty a full one instantly took its place of its own accord. The innkeeper stood in one corner and watched the affair; he did not at all know what to say, but thought, 'You could easily find a use for such a cook as that in your kitchen.'

The joiner and his comrades made merry until late into the night; at length they lay down to sleep, and the young apprentice also went to bed, and set his magic table against the wall.

The host's thoughts, however, let him have no rest; it occurred to him that there was a little old table in his lumber-room, which looked just like the apprentice's, and he brought it out quite softly, and exchanged it for the wishing-table.

Next morning the joiner paid for his bed, took up his table, never thinking that he had got a false one, and went his way. At mid-day he reached his father, who received him with great joy. 'Well, my dear son, what have you learnt?' said he to him.

'Father, I have become a joiner.'

'A good trade,' replied the old man, 'but what have you brought back with you from your apprenticeship?'

'Father, the best thing I have brought back with me is this little table.'

The tailor inspected it on all sides and said, 'You did not make a masterpiece when you made that; it is a bad old table.'

'It is a table which furnishes itself,' replied the son. 'When I set it out and tell it to cover itself, the most beautiful dishes stand on it, and a wine also, which gladdens the heart. Just invite all our relations and friends; they shall refresh and enjoy themselves for once, for the table will give them all they require.'

When the company was assembled, he put his table in the middle of the room and said, 'Little table, spread thyself,' but the little table did not bestir itself, and remained just as bare as any other table which did not understand language. Then the poor apprentice became aware that his table had been changed, and was ashamed at having to stand there like a liar. The relations, however, mocked him, and were forced to go home without having eaten or drunk. The father brought out his patches again, and went on tailoring, but the son went to a master in the craft.

The second son had gone to a miller and had apprenticed himself to him. When his years were over, the master said to him, 'As you have conducted yourself so well, I give you an ass of a peculiar kind, which neither draws a cart nor carries a sack.'

'To what use is he put, then?' asked the young apprentice.

'He lets gold drop from his mouth,' answered the miller. 'If you set him on a cloth and say "Bricklebrit", the good animal will drop gold-pieces for you.'

'That is a fine thing,' said the apprentice, and thanked the master, and went out into the world. When he had need of gold, he had only to say 'Bricklebrit' to his ass, and it rained gold-pieces, and he had nothing to do but pick them off the ground. Wheresoever he went, the best of everything was good enough for him, and the dearer the better, for he had always a full purse. When he had looked about the world for some time he thought, 'You must seek out your father; if you go to him with the gold-ass he will forget his anger and receive you well.'

It came to pass that he came to the same public-house in which his brother's table had been exchanged. He led his ass by the bridle, and the host was about to take the animal from him and tie him up, but the young apprentice said, 'Don't trouble yourself; I will take my grey horse into the stable, and tie him up myself, too, for I must know where he stands.'

This struck the host as odd, and he thought that a man who was forced to look after his ass himself could not have much to spend; but when the stranger put his hand in his pocket and brought out two gold-pieces, and said he was to provide something good for him, the host opened his eyes wide and ran and sought out the best he could muster.

After dinner the guest asked what he owed. The host did not see why he should not double the reckoning, and said the apprentice must give two more gold-pieces. He felt in his pocket, but his gold was just at an end. 'Wait an instant, sir host,' said he, 'I will go and fetch some money,' but he took the tablecloth with him. The host could not imagine what this could mean, and being curious, stole after him, and as the guest bolted the stable-door, he peeped through a hole left by a knot in the wood. The stranger spread out the cloth under the animal and cried, 'Bricklebrit', and immediately the beast began to let gold-pieces fall, so that it fairly rained down money on the ground.

'Eh, my word,' said the host, 'ducats are quickly coined there! A purse like that is not amiss.'

The guest paid his score and went to bed, but in the night the host stole down into the stable, led away the master of the mint, and tied up another ass in his place.

Early next morning the apprentice travelled away with the ass and thought that he had his gold-ass. At mid-day he reached his father, who rejoiced to see him again, and gladly took him in. 'What have you made of yourself, my son?' asked the old man.

'A miller, dear father,' he answered.

'What have you brought back with you from your travels?'

'Nothing else but an ass.'

'There are asses enough here,' said the father, 'I would rather have had a good goat.'

'Yes,' replied the son, 'but it is no common ass, but a gold-ass; when I say "Bricklebrit", the good beast opens its mouth and drops a whole sheetful of gold-pieces. Just summon all our relations hither, and I will make them rich folks.'

'That suits me well,' said the tailor, 'for then I shall have no need to torment myself any longer with the needle,' and ran out himself and called the relations together.

As soon as they were assembled, the miller bade them make way, spread out his cloth, and brought the ass into the room. 'Now watch,' said he, and cried 'Bricklebrit', but no gold-pieces fell, and it was clear that the animal knew nothing of the art, for every ass does not attain such perfection. Then the poor miller pulled a long face, saw that he was betrayed, and begged pardon of the relatives, who went home as poor as they came. There was no help for it—the old man had to betake him to his needle once more, and the youth hired himself to a miller.

The third brother had apprenticed himself to a turner, and, as that is skilled labour, he was the longest in learning. His brothers, however, told him in a letter how badly things had gone with them, and how the innkeeper had cheated them of their beautiful wishing-gifts on the last evening before they reached home. When the turner had served his time and had to set out on his travels, as he had conducted himself so well, his master presented him with a sack and said, 'There is a cudgel in it.'

'I can put on the sack,' said he, 'and it may be of good service to me, but why should the cudgel be in it? It only makes it heavy.'

'I will tell you why,' replied the master; 'if anyone has done anything to injure you, do but say, "Out of the sack, Cudgel!" and the cudgel will leap forth among the people and play such a dance on their backs that they will not be able to stir or move for a week, and it will not leave off until you say, "Into the sack, Cudgel!"'

The apprentice thanked him, put the sack on his back, and when any one came too near him, and wished to attack him, he said, 'Out of the sack, Cudgel!' and instantly the cudgel sprang out, and dusted the coat or the jacket of one after the other on their backs, and never stopped until it had stripped it off them, and it was done so quickly that before anyone was aware it was already his own turn.

In the evening the young turner reached the inn where his brothers had been cheated. He laid his sack on the table before him, and began to talk of all the wonderful things he had seen in the world. 'Yes,' said he, 'people may easily find a table which will cover itself, a gold-ass, and things of that kind—extremely good things which I by no means despise—but these are nothing in comparison to the treasure which I have won for myself and am carrying about with me in my sack here.'

The innkeeper pricked up his ears; 'What in the world can that be?' thought he. 'The sack must be filled with nothing but jewels. I ought to get them cheap, too, for all good things go in threes.'

When it was time for sleep, the guest stretched himself on the bench and laid his sack beneath him for a pillow. When the innkeeper thought his guest was lying in a sound sleep, he went to him, and pushed and pulled quite gently and carefully at the sack to see if he could possibly draw it away and lay another in its place. The turner had, however, been waiting for this for a long time, and now just as the innkeeper was about to give a hearty tug, he cried, 'Out of the sack, Cudgel!' Instantly the little cudgel came forth and fell on the innkeeper, and gave him a sound thrashing.

The host cried for mercy; but the louder he cried, so much the more heavily the cudgel beat the time on his back, until at length he fell to the ground exhausted. Then the turner said, 'If you do not give back the table which covers itself, and the gold-ass, the dance shall begin afresh.'

'Oh, no,' cried the host, quite humbly, 'I will gladly produce everything, only make the accursed kobold creep back into the sack.'

Then said the apprentice, 'I will let mercy take the place of justice, but beware of getting into mischief again!' So he cried, 'Into the sack, Cudgel!' and let him have rest.

Next morning the turner went home to his father with the wishing-table and the gold-ass. The tailor rejoiced when he saw him once more, and asked him likewise what he had learned in foreign parts. 'Dear father,' said he, 'I have become a turner.'

'A skilled trade,' said the father. 'What have you brought back with you from your travels?'

'A precious thing, dear father,' replied the son, 'a cudgel in the sack.'

'What!' cried the father, 'a cudgel! That's worth your trouble, indeed! From every tree you can cut yourself one.'

'But not one like this, dear father. If I say "Out of the sack, Cudgel!" the cudgel springs out and leads any one who means ill with me a weary dance, and never stops until he lies on the ground and prays for fair weather. Look you, with this cudgel have I got back the wishing-table and the gold-ass which the thievish innkeeper took away from my brothers. Now let them both be sent for, and invite all our kinsmen. I will give them to eat and to drink, and will fill their pockets with gold into the bargain.'

The old tailor would not quite believe him, but nevertheless got the relatives together. Then the turner spread a cloth in the room and led in the gold-ass, and said to his brother, 'Now, dear brother, speak to him.'

The miller said 'Bricklebrit', and instantly the gold-pieces fell down on the cloth like a thunder-shower, and the ass did not stop until everyone of them had so much that he could carry no more. (I can see in your face that you also would have liked to be there.)

Then the turner brought the little table, and said, 'Now, dear brother, speak to it.' And scarcely had the carpenter said, 'Table, spread thyself,' than it was spread and amply covered with the most exquisite dishes. Then such a meal took place as the good tailor had never yet known in his house, and the whole party of kinsmen stayed together till far in the night, and were all merry and glad. The tailor locked away needle and thread, yard-measure and goose, in a press, and lived with his three sons in joy and splendour.

What, however, became of the goat who was to blame for the tailor driving out his three sons? That I will tell you. She was ashamed that she had a bald head, and ran to a fox's hole, and crept into it. When the fox came home, he was met by two great eyes shining out of the darkness, and was terrified and ran away. A bear met him, and as the fox looked quite disturbed, he said, 'What is the matter with you, brother Fox, why do you look like that?'

'Ah,' answered Redskin, 'a fierce beast is in my cave and stared at me with its fiery eyes.'

30

'We will soon drive him out', said the bear, and went with him to the cave and looked in, but when he saw the fiery eyes, fear seized on him likewise; he would have nothing to do with the furious beast, and took to his heels.

The bee met him, and as she saw that he was ill at ease, she said, 'Bear, you are really pulling a very pitiful face; what has become of all your gaiety?'

'It is all very well for you to talk,' replied the bear. 'A furious beast with staring eyes is in Redskin's house, and we can't drive him out.'

The bee said, 'Bear, I pity you; I am a poor weak creature whom you would not turn aside to look at, but still, I believe I can help you.' She flew into the fox's cave, lighted on the goat's smoothly shorn head, and stung her so violently that she sprang up, crying 'Meh, meh,' and ran forth into the world as if mad, and to this hour no one knows where she has gone.

A poor peasant sat one evening by his hearth and poked the fire, while his wife sat opposite spinning. He said: 'What a sad thing it is that we have no children; our home is so quiet, while other folks' houses are noisy and cheerful.'

'Yes,' answered his wife, and she sighed; 'even if it were an only one, and if it were no bigger than my thumb, I should be quite content, and we would love it with all our hearts.'

Now some time after this, she had a little boy who was strong and healthy, but was no bigger than a thumb. Then they said: 'Our wish has been fulfilled, and, small as he is, we will love him dearly.' And because of his tiny stature they called him Tom Thumb. They let him want for nothing, yet the child grew no bigger, but remained the same size as when he was born. Still, he looked out on the world with intelligent eyes, and soon showed himself a clever and agile creature, who was lucky in all he attempted.

One day, when the peasant was preparing to go into the forest to cut wood, he said to himself, 'I wish I had someone to bring the cart after me.'

'Oh, father!' said Tom Thumb, 'I will soon bring it. You leave it to me; it shall be there at the appointed time.'

Then the peasant laughed, and said, 'How can that be? You are much too small even to hold the reins.'

'That doesn't matter, if only mother will harness the horse,' answered Tom. 'I will sit in his ear and tell him where to go.'

'Very well,' said the father, 'we will try it for once.'

When the time came, the mother harnessed the horse, set Tom in his ear, and then the little creature called out 'Gee-up' and 'Whoa' in turn, and directed the horse where to go. It went quite well, just as though it were being driven by its master; and they went the right way to the wood. Now it happened that while the cart was turning a corner, and Tom was calling to the horse, two strange men appeared on the scene.

'My goodness,' said one, 'what is this? There goes a cart, and a driver is calling to the horse, but there is nothing to be seen.'

'That is very peculiar,' said the other; 'we will follow the cart and see where it stops.'

The cart went on deep into the forest, and arrived quite safely at the place where the wood was cut.

When Tom spied his father, he said, 'You see, father, here I am with the cart;

now lift me down.' The father held the horse with his left hand, and took his little son out of its ear with the right. Then Tom sat down quite happily on a straw.

When the two strangers noticed him, they did not know what to say for astonishment.

Then one drew the other aside, and said: 'Listen, that little creature might make our fortune if we were to show him in the town for money. We will buy him.'

So they went up to the peasant, and said: 'Sell us the little man; he shall be well looked after with us.'

'No,' said the peasant, 'he is the delight of my eyes, and I will not sell him for all the gold in the world.'

But Tom Thumb, when he heard the bargain, crept up by the folds of his father's coat, placed himself on his shoulder, and whispered in his ear, 'Father, let me go; I will soon come back again.'

Then his father gave him to the two men for a fine piece of gold.

'Where will you sit?' they asked him.

'Oh, put me on the brim of your hat; then I can walk about and observe the neighbourhood without falling down.'

They did as he wished, and when Tom had said good-bye to his father, they went away with him.

They walked on till it was twilight, when the little man said, 'You must lift me down.'

'Stay where you are,' answered the man on whose head he sat.

'No,' said Tom, 'I will come down. Lift me down immediately.'

The man took off his hat and set the little creature in a field by the wayside. He jumped and crept about for a time, here and there among the sods, then slipped suddenly into a mouse-hole which he had discovered.

'Good evening, gentlemen, just you go home without me,' he called out to them in mockery.

They ran about and poked with sticks into the mouse-hole, but all in vain. Tom crept further and further back, and, as it soon got quite dark, they were forced to go home, full of anger and with empty purses.

When Tom noticed that they were gone, he crept out of his underground hiding-place again. 'It is dangerous walking in this field in the dark,' he said, 'one might easily break one's leg or one's neck.' Luckily, he came to an empty snail shell. 'Thank goodness,' he said, 'I can pass the night in safety here,' and he sat down.

Not long after, just when he was about to go to sleep, he heard two men pass by. One said: 'How shall we set about stealing the rich parson's gold and silver?'

'I can tell you,' interrupted Tom.

'What was that?' said one robber in a fright. 'I heard someone speak.'

They remained standing and listened.

Then Tom spoke again: 'Take me with you and I will help you.'

'Where are you?' they said.

'Just look on the ground and see where the voice comes from,' he answered.

At last the thieves found him, and lifted him up. 'You little urchin, are *you* going to help us?'

'Yes,' he said; 'I will creep between the iron bars in the pastor's room, and will hand out to you what you want.'

'All right,' they said, 'we will see what you can do.'

When they came to the parsonage, Tom crept into the room, but called out immediately with all his strength to the others: 'Do you want everything that is here?'

The thieves were frightened, and said, 'Do speak softly, and don't wake anyone.'

But Tom pretended not to understand, and called out again, 'What do you want? Everything?'

The cook, who slept above, heard him and sat up in bed and listened. But the thieves were so frightened that they retreated a little way. At last they summoned up courage again, and thought to themselves, 'The little rogue wants to tease us.' So they came back and whispered to him, 'Now, do be serious, and hand us out something.'

Then Tom called out again, as loud as he could, 'I will give you everything if only you will hold out your hands.'

The maid, who was listening intently, heard him quite distinctly and jumped out of bed and stumbled to the door. The thieves turned and fled, running as though wild huntsmen were after them. But the maid, seeing nothing, went to get a light. When she came back with it, Tom, unperceived, slipped out into the barn, and the maid, after she had searched every corner and found nothing, went to bed again thinking she had been dreaming with her eyes and ears open.

Tom Thumb climbed about in the hay, and found a splendid place to sleep. There he determined to rest till day came, and then to go home to his parents. But he had other experiences to go through first. Indeed, this world is full of trouble and sorrow!

The maid got up in the grey dawn to feed the cows. First she went into the barn, where she piled up an armful of hay, the very bundle in which poor Tom was asleep. But he slept so soundly that he knew nothing till he was almost in the mouth of the cow, who was eating him up with the hay.

'Heavens!' he said, 'however did I get into this mill?' But he soon saw where he was, and the great thing was to avoid being crushed between the cow's teeth. At last, whether he liked it or not, he had to go down the cow's throat.

'The windows have been forgotten in this house,' he said. 'The sun does not shine into it, and no light has been provided.'

Altogether he was very ill-pleased with his quarters, and, worst of all, more and more hay came in at the door, and the space grew narrower and narrower. At last he called out, in his fear, as loud as he could, 'Don't give me any more food. Don't give me any more food.'

The maid was just milking the cow, and when she heard the same voice as in the night, without seeing anyone, she was frightened and slipped from her stool and spilt the milk. Then, in the greatest haste, she ran to her master, and said: 'Oh Your Reverence, the cow has spoken!'

'You are mad,' he answered; but he went into the stable himself to see what was happening. Scarcely had he set foot in the cow-shed before Tom began again: 'Don't bring me any more food.'

Then the pastor was terrified too, and thought that the cow must be bewitched; so he ordered it to be killed. It was accordingly slaughtered, but the stomach, in which Tom was hidden, was thrown into the manure heap. Tom had the greatest trouble in working his way out. Just as he stuck out his head, a hungry wolf ran by and snapped up the whole stomach with one bite. But still Tom did not lose courage. 'Perhaps the wolf will listen to reason,' he said. So he called out, 'Dear wolf, I know where you could find a magnificent meal.'

'Where is it to be had?' asked the wolf.

'Why, in such and such a house,' answered Tom. 'You must squeeze through the grating of the store-room window, and there you will find cakes, bacon and sausages, as much as you can possibly eat.' And he went on to describe his father's house.

The wolf did not wait to hear this twice, and at night forced himself in through the grating and ate to his heart's content. When he was satisfied, he wanted to go away again; but he had grown so fat that he could not get out the same way. Tom had reckoned on this, and began to make a great commotion inside the wolf's body, struggling and screaming with all his might.

'Be quiet,' said the wolf, 'you will wake up the people of the house.'

'All very fine,' answered Tom. 'You have eaten your fill, and now I am going to make merry.' And he began to scream again with all his might.

At last his father and mother woke up, ran to the room, and looked through the crack of the door. When they saw a wolf, they went away, and the husband fetched his axe, and the wife a scythe.

'You stay behind,' said the man, as they came into the room. 'If my blow does not kill him, you must attack him and rip up his body.'

When Tom Thumb heard his father's voice, he called out: 'Dear father, I am here, inside the wolf's body.'

Full of joy, his father cried, 'Heaven be praised! Our dear child is found again,' and he bade his wife throw aside the scythe that it might not injure Tom.

Then he gathered himself together, and struck the wolf a blow on the head, so that it fell down lifeless. Then with knives and shears they ripped up the body, and took their little boy out.

'Ah,' said his father, 'how troubled we have been about you.'

'Yes, father, I have travelled about the world, and I am thankful to breathe fresh air again.'

'Wherever have you been?' they asked.

'Down a mouse-hole, in a cow's stomach and in a wolf's maw,' he answered; 'and now I shall stay with you.'

'And we will never sell you again, for all the riches in the world,' they said, kissing and fondling their dear child.

Then they gave him food and drink, and had new clothes made for him, as his own had been spoilt in his travels.

THE VALIANT TAILOR

A tailor was sitting on his table at the window one summer morning. He was a good fellow, and stitched with all his might. A peasant woman came down the street, crying, 'Good jam for sale! Good jam for sale!'

This had a pleasant sound in the tailor's ears; he put his pale face out of the window, and cried, 'You'll find a sale for your wares up here, good woman.'

The woman went up the three steps to the tailor, with the heavy basket on her head, and he made her unpack all her pots.

He examined them all, lifted them up, smelt them, and at last said, 'The jam

41

seems good; weigh me out four ounces, good woman, and should it come over the quarter pound, it will be all the same to me.'

The woman, who had hoped for a better sale, gave him what he asked for, but went away cross, and grumbling to herself.

'That jam will be a blessing to me,' cried the tailor; 'it will give me strength and power.' He brought his bread out of the cupboard, cut a whole slice, and spread the jam on it. 'It won't be a bitter morsel,' said he, 'but I will finish this waistcoat before I stick my teeth into it.'

He put the bread down by his side and went on with his sewing, but in his joy the stitches got bigger and bigger. The smell of the jam rose to the wall, where the flies were clustered in swarms, and tempted them to come down, and they settled on the jam in masses.

'Ah! who invited you?' cried the tailor, chasing away his unbidden guests. But the flies, who did not understand his language, were not to be got rid of so easily, and came back in greater numbers than ever. At last the tailor came to the end of his patience, and seizing a bit of cloth, he cried, 'Wait a bit, and I'll give it you!' So saying, he struck out at them mercilessly. When he looked, he found no fewer than seven dead and motionless. 'So that's the kind of fellow you are,' he said, admiring his own valour. 'The whole town shall know of this.'

In great haste he cut out a belt for himself, and stitched on it, in big letters: 'Seven at one blow!' 'The town,' he then said, 'the whole world shall know of it!' And his heart wagged for very joy like a lamb's tail. The tailor fastened the belt round his waist, and wanted to start out into the world at once; he found his workshop too small for his valour. Before starting, he searched the house to see if there was anything to take with him. He only found an old cheese, but this he put into his pocket. By the gate he saw a bird entangled in a thicket, and he put that into his pocket with the cheese. Then he boldly took to the road, and as he was light and active, he felt no fatigue. The road led up a mountain, and when he reached the highest point, he found a huge giant sitting there comfortably looking round him. The tailor went pluckily up to him, and addressed him.

'Good-day, comrade, you are sitting there surveying the wide world, I suppose. I am just on my way to try my luck. Do you feel inclined to go with me?'

The giant looked scornfully at the tailor, and said, 'You jackanapes! you miserable ragamuffin!'

'That may be,' said the tailor, unbuttoning his coat and showing the giant his belt. 'You may just read what kind of a fellow I am.'

The giant read, 'Seven at one blow,' and thought that it was people the tailor had slain; so it gave him a certain amount of respect for the little fellow. Still, he thought he would try him; so he picked up a stone and squeezed it till the water dropped out of it.

'Do that,' he said, 'if you have the strength.'

'No more than that?' said the tailor. 'Why, it's a mere joke to me.'

He put his hand into his pocket, and pulling out the bit of soft cheese, he squeezed it till the moisture ran out.

'I guess that will equal you,' said he.

The giant did not know what to say, and could not believe it of the little man.

Then the giant picked up a stone and threw it up so high that one could scarcely follow it with the eye.

'Now, then, you sample of a manikin, do that after me.'

'Well thrown!' said the tailor, 'but the stone fell to the ground again. Now I will throw one for you which will never come back at all.'

So saying, he put his hand into his pocket, took out the bird, and threw it into the air. The bird, overjoyed at its freedom, soared into the air and was never seen again.

'What do you think of that, comrade?' asked the tailor.

'You can certainly throw; but now we will see if you are in a condition to carry anything,' said the giant.

He led the tailor to a mighty oak which had been felled, and which lay upon the ground.

'If you are strong enough, help me out of the wood with this tree,' he said.

'Willingly,' answered the little man. 'You take the trunk on your shoulder, and I will take the branches; they must certainly be the heaviest.'

The giant accordingly took the trunk on his shoulder; but the tailor seated himself on one of the branches, and the giant, who could not look round, had to carry the whole tree, and the tailor into the bargain. The tailor was very merry on the end of the tree, and whistled 'Three tailors rode merrily out of the town,' as if tree-carrying were a joke to him.

When the giant had carried the tree some distance, he could go no further, and exclaimed, 'Look out, I am going to drop the tree!'

The tailor sprang to the ground with great agility, and seized the tree with both arms, as if he had been carrying it all the time. He said to the giant: 'Big fellow as you are, you can't carry a tree.'

After a time they went on together, and when they came to a cherry-tree the giant seized the top branches, where the cherries ripened first, bent them down, put them in the tailor's hand, and told him to eat. The tailor, however, was much too weak to hold the tree, and when the giant let go the tree sprang back, carrying the tailor with it into the air. When he reached the ground again without any injury, the giant said, 'What's this? Haven't you the strength to hold a feeble sapling?'

'It's not strength that's wanting,' answered the tailor. 'Do you think that would be anything to one who killed seven at a blow? I sprang over the tree because some sportsmen were shooting among the bushes. Spring after me if you like.'

The giant made the attempt, but he could not clear the tree, and stuck among the branches. So here, too, the tailor had the advantage of him.

The giant said, 'If you are such a gallant fellow, come with me to our cave and stay the night with us.'

The tailor was quite willing, and went with him. When they reached the cave, they found several other giants sitting round a fire, and each one held a roasted sheep in his hand, which he was eating. The tailor looked about him, and thought, 'It is much more roomy here than in my workshop.'

The giant showed him a bed and told him to lie down and have a good sleep. The bed was much too big for the tailor, so he did not lie down in it, but crept into a corner. At midnight, when the giant thought the tailor would be in a heavy sleep, he got up, took a big oak club, and with one blow crashed right through the bed, and thought he had put an end to the grasshopper. Early in the morning the giants went out into the woods, forgetting all about the tailor, when all at once he appeared before them, as lively as possible. They were terrified, and thinking he would strike them all dead, they ran off as fast as ever they could.

The tailor went on his way, always following his own pointed nose. When he had walked for a long time, he came to the courtyard of a royal palace. He was so tired that he lay down on the grass and went to sleep. While he lay and slept, the people came and inspected him on all sides, and they read on his belt, 'Seven at one blow.' 'Alas!' they said, 'why does this great warrior come here in time of peace? He must be a mighty man.'

They went to the King and told him about it; and they were of opinion that, should war break out, he would be a useful and powerful man who should on no account be allowed to depart. This advice pleased the King, and he sent one of his courtiers to the tailor to offer him a military appointment when he woke up. The messenger remained standing by the tailor, till he opened his eyes and stretched himself, and then he made the offer.

'For that very purpose have I come,' said the tailor. 'I am quite ready to enter the King's service.'

So he was received with honour, and a special dwelling was assigned to him.

The soldiers, however, bore him a grudge, and wished him a thousand miles away. 'What will be the end of it?' they said to each other. 'When we quarrel with him, and he strikes out, seven of us will fall at once. One of us can't cope with him.' So they took a resolve, and went all together to the King, and asked for their discharge. 'We are not made,' said they, 'to hold our own with a man who strikes seven at one blow.'

It grieved the King to lose all his faithful servants for the sake of one man;

he wished he had never set eyes on the tailor, and was quite ready to let him go. He did not dare, however, to give him his dismissal, for he was afraid that he would kill him and all his people, and place himself on the throne. He pondered over it for a long time, and at last he thought of a plan. He sent for the tailor, and said that as he was so great a warrior he would make him an offer. In a forest in his kingdom lived two giants, who, by robbery, murder, burning and laying waste, did much harm. No one dared approach them without being in danger of his life. If he could subdue and kill these two giants, he would give him his only daughter to be his wife, and half his kingdom as a dowry; also he would give him a hundred horsemen to accompany and help him.

'That would be something for a man like me,' thought the tailor. 'A beautiful princess and half a kingdom are not offered to one every day.'

'Oh, yes,' was his answer, 'I will soon subdue the giants, and that without the hundred horsemen. He who slays seven at one blow need not fear two.'

The tailor set out at once, accompanied by the hundred horsemen; but when he came to the edge of the forest, he said to his followers, 'Wait here, I will soon make an end of the giants by myself.'

Then he disappeared into the wood; he looked about to the right and to the left. Before long he espied both the giants lying under a tree fast asleep, and snoring. Their snores were so tremendous that they made the branches of the tree dance up and down. The tailor, who was no fool, filled his pockets with stones and climbed up the tree. When he got half-way up, he slipped on to a branch just above the sleepers, and then hurled the stones, one after another, on to one of them.

It was some time before the giant noticed anything; then he woke up, pushed his companion, and said, 'What are you hitting me for?'

'You're dreaming,' said the other, 'I didn't hit you.' They went to sleep again, and the tailor threw a stone at the other one. 'What's that?' he cried. 'What are you throwing at me?'

'I'm not throwing anything,' answered the first one, with a growl.

They quarrelled over it for a time, but as they were sleepy, they made it up, and their eyes closed again.

The tailor began his game once more, picked out his biggest stone, and threw it at the first giant as hard as he could.

'This is too bad,' said the giant, flying up like a madman. He pushed his companion against the tree with such violence that it shook. The other paid him back in the same coin, and they worked themselves up into such a rage that they tore up trees by the roots, and hacked at each other till they both fell dead upon the ground.

Then the tailor jumped down from his perch. 'It was very lucky,' he said, 'that they did not tear up the tree I was sitting on, or I should have had to spring on to another like a squirrel; but we tailors are nimble fellows.' He drew his sword, and gave each of the giants two or three cuts in the chest. Then he went out to the horsemen, and said, 'The work is done. I have given both of them the finishing stroke, but it was a difficult job. In their distress they tore trees up by the roots to defend themselves; but all that's no good when a man like me comes, who slays seven at one blow.'

'Are you not wounded?' asked the horseman.

'There was no danger,' answered the tailor. 'Not a hair of my head was touched.'

The horsemen would not believe him, and rode into the forest to see. There, right enough, lay the giants in pools of blood, and, round about them, the uprooted trees.

The tailor now demanded his reward from the King; but he, in the meantime, had repented of his promise, and was again trying to think of a plan to shake him off.

'Before I give you my daughter and the half of my kingdom, you must perform one more doughty deed. There is a unicorn which runs about in the forests doing vast damage; you must capture it.'

'I have even less fear of one unicorn than of two giants. Seven at one stroke is my style.'

He took a rope and an axe and went into the wood, and told his followers to stay outside. He did not have long to wait. The unicorn soon appeared, and dashed towards the tailor as if it meant to run him through with its horn on the spot. 'Softly, softly,' cried the tailor. 'Not so fast.' He stood still, and waited till the animal got quite near, and then he very nimbly dodged behind a tree. The unicorn rushed at the tree and ran its horn so hard into the trunk that it had not strength to pull it out again, and so it was caught.

'Now I have the prey,' said the tailor, coming from behind the tree. He fastened the rope round the creature's neck, and, with his axe, released the horn from the tree. When this was done he led the animal away and took it to the King.

Still the King would not give him the promised reward, but made a third demand of him. Before the marriage, the tailor must catch a boar which did much damage in the woods; the huntsmen were to help him.

'Willingly,' said the tailor. 'That will be mere child's play.'

He did not take the huntsmen into the wood with him, at which they were well pleased, for they had already more than once had such a reception from the boar that they had no wish to encounter him again. When the boar saw the tailor, it flew at him with foaming mouth, and, gnashing its teeth, tried to throw him to the ground; but the nimble hero darted into a little chapel which stood near. He jumped out again immediately by the window. The boar rushed in after the tailor; but the latter by this time was hopping about outside and quickly shut the door upon the boar. So the raging animal was caught, for it was far too heavy and clumsy to jump out of the window. The tailor called the huntsmen up to see the captive with their own eyes.

The hero then went to the King, who was now obliged to keep his word, whether he liked it or not; so he handed over his daughter and half his kingdom to him. Had he known that it was no warrior but only a tailor who stood before him, he would have taken it even more to heart. The marriage was held with much pomp, but little joy, and a King was made out of a tailor.

After a time the young Queen heard her husband talking in his sleep and saying, 'Apprentice, bring me the waistcoat, and patch the trousers, or I will break the yard-measure over your head.' So in this manner she discovered the young gentleman's origin. In the morning she complained to the King, and begged him to rid her of a husband who was nothing more than a tailor.

The King comforted her, and said, 'Tonight, leave your bedroom door open. My servants shall stand outside, and when he is asleep they shall go in and bind him. They shall then carry him off and put him on board a ship which will take him far away.'

The lady was satisfied with this; but the tailor's armour-bearer, who was attached to his young lord, told him the whole plot.

'I will put a stop to their plan,' said the tailor.

At night he went to bed as usual with his wife. When she thought he was asleep, she got up, opened the door, and lay down again. The tailor, who had only pretended to be asleep, began to cry out in a clear voice: 'Apprentice, bring me the waistcoat, and patch the trousers, or I will break the yard-measure over your head. I have slain seven at one blow, killed two giants, led captive a unicorn and caught a boar; should I be afraid of those who are standing outside my chamber door?'

When they heard the tailor speaking like this, the servants were overcome by fear and ran away as if wild animals were after them, and none of them would venture near him again.

So the tailor remained a King till the day of his death.

THE SIX SWANS

Once upon a time, a certain King was hunting in a great forest, and he chased a wild beast so eagerly that none of his attendants could follow him. When evening drew near he stopped and looked around him, and then he saw that he had lost his way.

He sought a way out but could find none. Then he perceived an aged woman with a head which nodded perpetually, who came towards him, but she was a witch. 'Good woman,' said he to her, 'can you not show me the way through the forest?'

'Oh yes, Lord King,' she answered, 'that I certainly can, but on one condition, and if you do not fulfil that, you will never get out of the forest and will die of hunger in it.'

'What kind of condition is it?' asked the King.

'I have a daughter,' said the old woman, 'who is as beautiful as anyone in the world, and well deserves to be your consort, and if you will make her your Queen, I will show you the way out of the forest.'

In the anguish of his heart the King consented, and the old woman led him to her little hut, where her daughter was sitting by the fire. She received the King as if she had been expecting him, and he saw that she was very beautiful, but still she did not please him, and he could not look at her without secret horror. After he had taken the maiden up on his horse, the old woman showed him the way, and the King reached his royal palace again, where the wedding was celebrated.

The King had already been married once, and had, by his first wife, seven children, six boys and a girl, whom he loved better than anything else in the world. As he now feared that the stepmother might not treat them well, and even do them some injury, he took them to a lonely castle which stood in the midst of a forest. It lay so concealed, and the way was so difficult to find, that he himself would not have found it, if a wise woman had not given him a ball of yarn with wonderful properties. When he threw it down before him, it unrolled itself and showed him the path.

The King, however, went so frequently away to his dear children that the Queen observed his absence; she was curious and wanted to know what he did when he was quite alone in the forest. She gave a great deal of money to his servants, and they betrayed the secret to her, and told her likewise of the ball which alone could point out the way. And now she knew no rest until she had learnt where the King kept the ball of yarn; and then she made little shirts of white silk, and as she had learnt the art of witchcraft from her mother, she sewed a charm inside them. And once, when the King had ridden forth to hunt, she took the little shirts and went into the forest, and the ball showed her the way.

The children, who saw from a distance that someone was approaching, thought that their dear father was coming, and full of joy, ran to meet him. Then she threw one of the little shirts over each of them, and no sooner had the shirts touched their bodies than they were changed into swans, and flew away over the forest.

The Queen went home quite delighted, and thought she had got rid of her step-children, but the girl had not run out with her brothers, and the Queen knew nothing about her. Next day the King went to visit his children, but he found no one but the little girl. 'Where are your brothers?' asked the King.

'Alas, dear father,' she answered, 'they have gone away and left me alone!' and she told him that she had seen from her little window how her brothers had

49

flown away over the forest in the shape of swans, and she showed him the feathers, which they had let fall in the courtyard, and which she had picked up. The King mourned, but he did not think that the Queen had done this wicked deed, and as he feared that the girl would also be stolen away from him, he wanted to take her away with him. But she was afraid of her stepmother and entreated the King to let her stay just this one night more in the forest castle.

The poor girl thought, 'I can no longer stay here. I will go and seek my brothers.' And when night came, she ran away and went straight into the forest. She walked the whole night long, and next day also without stopping, until she could go no farther for weariness. Then she saw a forest-hut, and went into it, and found a room with six little beds, but she did not venture to get into any of them, but crept under one and lay down on the hard ground, intending to pass the night there. Just before sunset, however, she heard a rustling and saw six swans come flying into the window. They alighted on the ground and blew at each other, and blew all the feathers off, and their swans' skins stripped off like a shirt. Then the maiden looked at them and recognised her brothers, was glad and crept forth from beneath the bed. The brothers were not less delighted to see their little sister, but their joy was of short duration.

'Here you cannot abide,' they said to her. 'This is a shelter for robbers; if they come home and find you, they will kill you.'

'But can you not protect me?' asked the little sister.

'No,' they replied, 'only for one quarter of an hour each evening can we lay aside our swans' skins and have during that time our human form; after that, we are once more turned into swans.'

The little sister wept, and said, 'Can you not be set free?'

'Alas, no,' they answered, 'the conditions are too hard! For six years you may neither speak nor laugh, and in that time you must sew together six little shirts of starwort for us. And if one single word falls from your lips, all your work will be lost.' And when the brothers had said this, the quarter of an hour was over, and they flew out of the window again as swans.

The maiden, however, firmly resolved to deliver her brothers, even if it should cost her her life. She left the hut, went into the midst of the forest, seated herself on a tree, and there passed the night. Next morning she went out and gathered starwort and began to sew. She could not speak to anyone, and she had no inclination to laugh; she sat there and looked at nothing but her work.

When she had already spent a long time there it came to pass that the King of the country was hunting in the forest, and his huntsmen came to the tree on which the maiden was sitting. They called to her and said, 'Who art thou?' But she made no answer. 'Come down to us,' said they, 'we will not do thee any harm.' She only shook her head. As they pressed her further with questions she threw her gold necklace down to them, and thought to content them thus. They, however, did not cease, and then she threw her girdle down to them, and as this also was to no purpose, her garters, and by degrees everything that she had on that she could do without until she had nothing left but her shift. The huntsmen, however, did not let themselves be turned aside by that, but climbed the tree and fetched the maiden down, and led her before the King.

The King asked, 'Who art thou? What art thou doing on the tree?'

But she did not answer. He put the question in every language that he knew, but she remained as mute as a fish. As she was so beautiful, the King's heart was touched, and he was smitten with a great love for her. He put his mantle on her, took her before him on his horse, and carried her to his castle. Then he caused her to be dressed in rich garments, and she shone in her beauty like great daylight, but no word could be drawn from her. He placed her by his side at table, and her modest bearing and courtesy pleased him so much that he said, 'She is the one whom I wish to marry, and no other woman in the world.' And after some days he united himself to her.

The King, however, had a wicked mother who was dissatisfied with this marriage and spoke ill of the young Queen. 'Who knows,' said she, 'from whence the creature who can't speak comes? She is not worthy of a king!'

After a year had passed, when the Queen brought her first child into the world, the old woman took it away from her and smeared her mouth with blood as she slept. Then she went to the King and accused the Queen of being a man-eater. The King would not believe it, and would not suffer anyone to do her any injury. She, however, sat continually sewing at the shirts, and cared for nothing else.

The next time, when she again bore a beautiful boy, the false stepmother used the same treachery, but the King could not bring himself to give credit to her words. He said, 'She is too pious and good to do anything of that kind; if she were not dumb and could defend herself, her innocence would come to light.'

But when the old woman stole away the newly-born child for the third time, and accused the Queen, who did not utter one word of self-defence, the King could do no otherwise than deliver her over to justice, and she was sentenced to suffer death by fire.

When the day came for the sentence to be executed, it was the last day of the six years during which she was not to speak or laugh, and she had delivered her dear brothers from the power of the enchantment. The six shirts were ready, only the left sleeve of the sixth was wanting. When, therefore, she was led to the stake, she laid the shirts on her arm, and when she stood on high and the fire was just going to be lighted, she looked around and six swans came flying through the air towards her. Then she saw that her deliverance was near, and her heart leapt with joy. The swans swept towards her and sank down so that she could throw the shirts over them, and as they were touched by them their swans' skins fell off, and her brothers stood in their own bodily form before her, and were vigorous and handsome. The youngest only lacked his left arm, and had in the place of it a swan's wing on his shoulder. They embraced and kissed each other, and the Queen went to the King, who was greatly moved, and she began to speak and said, 'Dearest husband, now I may speak and declare to thee that I am innocent, and falsely accused.' And she told of the treachery of the old woman who had taken away her three children and hidden them. Then to the great joy of the King they were brought thither, and, as a punishment, the wicked mother was bound to the stake and burnt to ashes. But the King and the Queen with the six brothers lived many years in happiness and peace.

THE SPIRIT IN THE BOTTLE

There was once a poor woodcutter who toiled from early morning till late night. When at last he had laid by some money he said to his boy, 'You are my only child; I will spend the money which I have earned by the sweat of my brow on your education. If you learn some honest trade you can support me in my old age, when my limbs have grown stiff and I am obliged to stay at home.'

Then the boy went to a high school and learned diligently so that his masters praised him, and he remained there a long time. When he had worked through two classes, but was still not yet perfect in everything, the little pittance which the father had earned was all spent, and the boy was obliged to return home to him.

'Ah,' said the father sorrowfully, 'I can give you no more, and in these hard times I cannot earn a farthing more than will suffice for our daily bread.'

'Dear father,' answered the son, 'don't trouble yourself about it; if it is God's will it will turn to my advantage. I shall soon accustom myself to it.'

When the father wanted to go into the forest to earn money by helping to pile and stack wood and also to chop it, the son said, 'I will go with you and help you.'

'Nay, my son,' said the father, 'that would be hard for you; you are not accustomed to rough work, and will not be able to bear it, besides I have only one axe and no money left wherewith to buy another.'

'Just go to the neighbour,' answered the son. 'He will lend you an axe until I have earned one for myself.'

The father then borrowed an axe of the neighbour, and next morning at break of day they went out into the forest together. The son helped his father and was quite merry and brisk about it. But when the sun was right over their heads, the father said, 'We will rest and have our dinner, and then we shall work as well again.'

The son took his bread in his hands and said, 'Just you rest, father, I am not tired; I will walk up and down a little in the forest, and look for birds' nests.'

'Oh, you fool,' said the father, 'why should you want to run about there? Afterwards you will be tired, and no longer able to raise your arm; stay here, and sit down beside me.'

The son, however, went into the forest, ate his bread, was very merry, and peered in among the green branches to see if he could discover a bird's nest anywhere. So he went up and down until at last he came to a great dangerous-looking oak, which certainly was already many hundred years old, and which five men could not have spanned. He stood still and looked at it, and thought, 'Many a bird must have built its nest in that.'

Then all at once it seemed to him that he heard a voice. He listened and became aware that someone was crying in a very smothered voice, 'Let me out! Let me out!' He looked around but could discover nothing; nevertheless, he fancied that the voice came out of the ground.

Then he cried, 'Where are you?'

The voice answered, 'I am here down amongst the roots of the oak-tree. Let me out! Let me out!'

The scholar began to loosen the earth under the tree and search among the roots, until at last he found a glass bottle in a little hollow. He lifted it up and held it against the light, and then saw a creature shaped like a frog springing up and down in it.

'Let me out! Let me out!' it cried anew, and the scholar, thinking no evil, drew the cork out of the bottle. Immediately a spirit ascended from it, and began

54

to grow, and grew so fast that in a very few moments he stood before the scholar, a terrible fellow as big as half the tree by which he was standing.

'Know you,' he cried in an awful voice, 'what your wages are for having let me out?'

'No,' replied the scholar fearlessly, 'how should I know that?'

'Then I will tell you,' cried the spirit; 'I must strangle you for it.'

'You should have told me that sooner,' said the scholar, 'for I should then have left you shut up, but my head shall stand fast for all you can do; more persons than one must be consulted about that.'

'More persons here, more persons there,' said the spirit. 'You shall have the wages you have earned. Do you think that I was shut up there for such a long time as a favour? No, it was a punishment for me. I am the mighty Mercurius. Whoso releases me, him must I strangle.'

'Softly,' answered the scholar, 'not so fast. I must first know that you really were shut up in that little bottle, and that you are the right spirit. If, indeed, you can get in again, I will believe, and then you may do as you will with me.'

The spirit said haughtily, 'That is a very trifling feat,' drew himself together, and made himself as small and slender as he had been at first, so that he crept through the same opening, and right through the neck of the bottle in again. Scarcely was he within than the scholar thrust the cork he had drawn back into the bottle, and threw it among the roots of the oak into its old place, and the spirit was betrayed.

And now the scholar was about to return to his father, but the spirit cried very piteously. 'Ah, do let me out! Ah, do let me out!'

'No,' answered the scholar, 'not a second time! He who has once tried to take my life shall not be set free by me, now that I have caught him again.'

'If you will set me free,' said the spirit, 'I will give you so much that you will have plenty all the days of your life.'

'No,' answered the scholar, 'you would cheat me as you did the first time.'

'You are playing away your own good luck,' said the spirit; 'I will do you no harm, but will reward you richly.'

The scholar thought, 'I will venture it; perhaps he will keep his word, and anyhow he shall not get the better of me.'

Then he took out the cork, and the spirit rose up from the bottle as he had done before, stretched himself out and became as big as a giant.

'Now you shall have your reward,' said he, and handed the scholar a little bag just like a plaster, and said, 'If you spread one end of this over a wound it will heal, and if you rub steel or iron with the other end it will be changed into silver.'

'I must try that,' said the scholar, and went to a tree, tore off the bark with his axe, and rubbed it with one end of the plaster. It immediately closed together and was healed. 'Now it is all right,' he said to the spirit, 'and we can part.' The spirit thanked him for his release, and the scholar thanked the spirit for his present, and went back to his father.

'Where have you been racing about?' said the father; 'why have you forgotten your work? I said at once that you would never get on with anything.'

'Be easy, father, I will make it up.'

'Make it up, indeed,' said the father angrily, 'there's no art in that.'

'Take care, father, I will soon hew that tree there, so that it will split.'

Then he took his plaster, rubbed the axe with it, and dealt a mighty blow, but as the iron had changed into silver, the edge turned. 'Hullo, father, just look what a bad axe you've given me; it has become quite crooked.'

The father was shocked, and said, 'Ah, what have you done? Now I shall have to pay for that, and have not the wherewithal, and that is all the good I have got by your work.'

'Don't get angry,' said the son, 'I will soon pay for the axe.'

'Oh, you blockhead,' cried the father, 'how will you pay for it? You have nothing but what I give you. These are students' tricks that are sticking in your head, but you have no idea of wood-cutting.'

After a while the scholar said, 'Father, I can really work no more; we had better take a holiday.'

'Eh, what!' answered he. 'Do you think I will sit with my hands lying in my lap like you? I must go on working, but you may take yourself off home.'

'Father, I am here in this wood for the first time; I don't know my way alone. Do go with me.'

As his anger had now abated, the father at last let himself be persuaded and went home with him. Then he said to the son, 'Go and sell your damaged axe, and see what you can get for it, and I must earn the difference, in order to pay the neighbour.'

The son took the axe and carried it into town to a goldsmith, who tested it, laid it in the scales, and said, 'It is worth four hundred thalers; I have not so much as that by me.'

The son said, 'Give me what you have; I will lend you the rest.'

The goldsmith gave him three hundred thalers, and remained a hundred in his debt. The son thereupon went home and said, 'Father, I have got the money; go and ask the neighbour what he wants for the axe.'

'I know that already,' answered the old man, 'one thaler, six groschen.'

'Then give him two thalers, twelve groschen—that is double and enough; see, I have money in plenty,' and he gave the father a hundred thalers, and said, 'You shall never know want; live as comfortably as you like.'

'Good heavens!' said the father, 'how have you come by these riches?'

The scholar then told how all had come to pass, and how he, trusting in his luck, had made such a good hit. But with the money that was left, he went back to the high school and went on learning more, and as he could heal all wounds with his plaster, he became the most famous doctor in the whole world.

A rich farmer was one day standing in his yard inspecting his fields and gardens. The corn was growing up vigorously and the fruit-trees were heavily laden with fruit. The grain of the year before still lay in such immense heaps on the floors that the rafters could hardly bear it. Then he went into the stable, where were well-fed oxen, fat cows and horses bright as looking-glass. At length, he went back into his sitting-room, and cast a glance at the iron chest in which his money lay.

Whilst he was thus standing surveying his riches, all at once there was a loud knock close by him. The knock was not at the door of his room, but at the door of his heart. It opened, and he heard a voice which said to him, 'Have you done good to your family with it? Have you considered the necessities of the poor? Have you shared your bread with the hungry? Have you been contented with what you have, or did you always desire to have more?'

The heart was not slow in answering, 'I have been hard and pitiless, and have never shown any kindness to my own family. If a beggar came, I turned away my eyes from him. I have not troubled myself about God, but have thought only of increasing my wealth. If everything which the sky covers had been my own, I should still not have had enough.'

When he was aware of this answer he was greatly alarmed, his knees began to tremble, and he was forced to sit down.

Then there was another knock, but the knock was at the door of his room. It was his neighbour, a poor man who had a number of children whom he could no longer satisfy with food. 'I know,' thought the poor man, 'that my neighbour is rich, but he is as hard as he is rich. I don't believe he will help me, but my children are crying for bread, so I will venture it.' He said to the rich man, 'You do not readily give away anything that is yours, but I stand here like one who feels the water rising above his head. My children are starving; lend me four measures of corn.'

The rich man looked at him long, and then the first sunbeam of mercy began to melt away a drop of the ice of greediness. 'I will not lend you four measures,' he answered, 'but I will make you a present of eight, if you fulfil one condition.'

'What am I to do?' said the poor man.

'When I am dead, you shall watch for three nights by my grave.'

The peasant was disturbed in his mind at this request, but in the need in which he was, he would have consented to anything; he accepted, therefore, and carried the corn home with him.

It seemed as if the rich man had foreseen what was about to happen, for when three days were gone by, he suddenly dropped down dead. No one knew exactly how it came to pass, but no one grieved for him. When he was buried, the poor man remembered his promise; he would willingly have been released from it, but he thought, 'After all, he acted kindly by me. I have fed my hungry children with his corn, and even if that were not the case, where I have once given my promise I must keep it.'

At nightfall, he went into the churchyard, and seated himself on the grave-mound. Everything was quiet; only the moon appeared above the grave, and frequently an owl flew past and uttered her melancholy cry. When the sun rose, the poor man betook himself in safety to his home, and in the same manner the second night passed quietly by. On the evening of the third day he felt a strange uneasiness; it seemed to him that something was about to happen. When he went out he saw, by the churchyard wall, a man whom he had never seen before. He was no longer young, had scars on his face, and his eyes looked sharply and eagerly around. He was entirely covered with an old cloak, and nothing was visible but his great riding-boots. 'What are you looking for here?' asked the peasant. 'Are you not afraid of the lonely churchyard?'

'I am looking for nothing,' he answered, 'and I am afraid of nothing! I am like the story of the youth who went forth to learn how to shudder, and knew no fear. But he got the King's daughter to wife and great wealth with her, and I remain poor. I am nothing but a paid-off soldier, and I mean to pass the night here, because I have no other shelter.'

'If you are without fear,' said the peasant, 'stay with me, and help me to watch that grave there.'

'To keep watch is a soldier's business,' he replied; 'whatever we fall in with here, whether it be good or bad, we will share it between us.' The peasant agreed to this and they seated themselves on the grave together.

All was quiet until midnight, when suddenly a shrill whistling was heard in the air, and the two watchers perceived the Evil One standing bodily before them.

'Be off, you ragamuffins!' cried he to them, 'the man who lies in that grave belongs to me; I want to take him, and if you don't go away I will wring your necks!'

'Sir with the red feather,' said the soldier, 'you are not my captain, I have no need to obey you, and I have not yet learned how to fear. Go away, we shall stay sitting here.'

The Devil thought to himself, 'Money is the best thing with which to get hold of these two vagabonds.' So he began to play a softer tune, and asked quite kindly if they would not accept a bag of money and go home with it.

'That is worth listening to,' said the soldier, 'but one bag of gold won't serve us;

if you will give as much as will go into one of my boots, we will quit the field for you and go away.'

'I have not so much as that about me,' said the Devil, 'but I will fetch it. In the neighbouring town lives a money-changer who is a good friend of mine, and will readily advance it to me.'

When the Devil had vanished the soldier took his left boot off, and said, 'We will soon pull the charcoal-burner's nose for him; just give me your knife, comrade.' He cut the sole off the boot, and put it in the high grass near the grave on the edge of a hole that was half overgrown. 'That will do,' said he; 'now the chimney-sweep may come.'

They both sat down and waited, and it was not long before the Devil returned with a small bag of gold in his hand.

'Just pour it in,' said the soldier, raising up the boot a little, 'but that won't be enough.'

The Black One shook out all that was in the bag; the gold fell through and the boot remained empty. 'Stupid Devil,' cried the soldier, 'it won't do! Didn't I say so at once? Go back again and bring more.'

The Devil shook his head, went, and in an hour's time came with a much larger bag under his arm.

'Now pour it in,' cried the soldier, 'but I doubt the boot will be full.' The gold clinked as it fell, but the boot remained empty. The Devil looked in himself with his burning eyes, and convinced himself of the truth.

'You have shamefully big calves to your legs!' cried he, and made a wry face.

'Do you think,' replied the soldier, 'that I have a cloven foot like you? Since when have you been so stingy? See that you get more gold together, or our bargain will come to nothing!'

The Wicked One went off again. This time he stayed away longer, and when at length he appeared he was panting under the weight of a sack which lay on his shoulders. He emptied it into the boot, which was just as far from being filled as before. He became furious, and was just going to tear the boot out of the soldier's hands, but at that moment the first ray of the rising sun broke forth from the sky, and the Evil Spirit fled away with loud shrieks. The poor soul was saved.

The peasant wished to divide the gold, but the soldier said, 'Give what falls to my lot to the poor. I will come with thee to thy cottage, and together we will live in rest and peace on what remains, as long as God is pleased to permit.'

THE MASTER-THIEF

One day an old man and his wife were sitting in front of a miserable house resting a while from their work. Suddenly a splendid carriage with four black horses came driving up, and a richly-dressed man descended from it. The peasant stood up, went to the great man, and asked what he wanted, and in what way he could be useful to him. The stranger stretched out his hand to the old man, and said, 'I want nothing but to enjoy for once a country dish; cook me some potatoes in the way you always have them, and then I will sit down at your table and eat them with pleasure.'

The peasant smiled and said, 'You are a count or a prince, or perhaps even a duke; noble gentlemen often have such fancies, but you shall have your wish.'

The wife went into the kitchen and began to wash and rub the potatoes, and to make them into balls, as they are eaten by the country-folks. Whilst she was busy with this work, the peasant said to the stranger, 'Come into my garden with me for a while; I have still something to do there.' He had dug some holes in the garden and now wanted to plant some trees in them.

'Have you no children,' asked the stranger, 'who could help you with your work?'

'No,' answered the peasant, 'I had a son, it is true, but it is long since he went out into the world. He was a ne'er-do-well, sharp and knowing, but he would learn nothing and was full of bad tricks. At last he ran away from me, and since then I have heard nothing of him.'

The old man took a young tree, put it in a hole, drove in a post beside it, and when he had shovelled in some earth and had trampled it firmly down, he tied the stem of the tree above, below, and in the middle, fast to the post by a rope of straw.

'But tell me,' said the stranger, 'why don't you tie that crooked knotted tree, which is lying in the corner there bent down almost to the ground, to a post also that it may grow straight as well as these?'

The old man smiled and said, 'Sir, you speak according to your knowledge; it is easy to see that you are not familiar with gardening. That tree there is old and mis-shapen; no one can make it straight now. Trees must be trained while they are young.'

'That is how it was with your son,' said the stranger; 'if you had trained him while he was still young, he would not have run away. Now he, too, must have grown hard and mis-shapen.'

'Truly it is a long time since he went away,' replied the old man, 'he must have changed.'

'Would you know him again if he were to come to you?' asked the stranger.

'Hardly by his face,' replied the peasant, 'but he has a mark about him, a birthmark on his shoulder, that looks like a bean.'

When he said that the stranger pulled off his coat, bared his shoulder, and showed the peasant the bean.

'Good God!' cried the old man, 'thou art really my son!' and love for his child stirred in his heart. 'But,' he added, 'how canst thou be my son? Thou hast become a great lord and livest in wealth and luxury. How hast thou contrived to do that?'

'Ah, father,' answered the son, 'the young tree was bound to no post and has grown crooked; now it is too old—it will never be straight again. How have I got all that? I have become a thief; but do not be alarmed, I am a master-thief. For me there are neither locks nor bolts; whatsoever I desire is mine. Do not imagine that I steal like a common thief; I only take some of the superfluity of the rich. Poor people are safe—I would rather give to them than take anything from them. It is the same with anything which I can have without trouble, cunning and dexterity—I never touch it.'

'Alas, my son,' said the father, 'it still does not please me. A thief is still a thief; I tell thee it will end badly.'

He took him to his mother, and when she heard that this was her son, she wept for joy, but when he told her that he had become a master-thief, two streams flowed down over her face. At length she said, 'Even if he has become a thief, he is still my son, and my eyes have beheld him once more.'

They sat down to table, and once again he ate with his parents the wretched food which he had not eaten for so long.

The father said, 'If our lord, the count up there in the castle, learns who thou art and what trade thou followest, he will not take thee in his arms and cradle thee in them as he did when he held thee at the font, but will cause thee to swing from a halter.'

'Be easy, father, he will do me no harm, for I understand my trade. I will go to him myself this very day.'

When evening drew near, the master-thief seated himself in his carriage and drove to the castle. The count received him civilly, for he took him for a distinguished man. When, however, the stranger made himself known, the count turned pale and was quite silent for some time. At length he said, 'You are my godson, and on that account mercy shall take the place of justice, and I will deal leniently with you. Since you pride yourself on being a master-thief, I will put your art to the proof, but if you do not stand the test, you must marry the ropemaker's daughter, and the croaking of the raven must be your music on the occasion.'

'Lord Count,' answered the master-thief, 'think of three things, as difficult as you like, and if I do not perform your tasks, do with me what you will.'

The count reflected for some minutes, and then said, 'Well, then, in the first place, you shall steal the horse I keep for my own riding out of the stable; in the next, you shall steal the sheet from beneath the bodies of my wife and myself when we are asleep, without our observing it, and the wedding-ring of my wife as well; thirdly and lastly, you shall steal away out of the church the parson and clerk. Mark what I am saying, for your life depends on it.'

The master-thief went to the nearest town; there he bought the clothes of an old peasant-woman, and put them on. Then he stained his face brown and painted wrinkles on it as well, so that no one could have recognised him. Then he filled a small cask with old Hungary wine in which was mixed a powerful sleeping-drink. He put the cask in a basket, which he took on his back, and walked with slow and tottering steps to the count's castle.

It was already dark when he arrived. He sat down on a stone in the courtyard and began to cough like an asthmatic old woman, and to rub his hands as if he were cold. In front of the door of the stable some soldiers were lying round a fire; one of them observed the woman, and called out to her, 'Come nearer, old mother, and warm yourself beside us. After all, you have no bed for the night, and must take one where you can find it.'

The old woman tottered up to them, begged them to lift the basket from her back, and sat down beside them at the fire.

'What have you got in your cask, old lady?' asked one.

'A good mouthful of wine,' she answered. 'I live by trade; for money and fair words I am quite ready to let you have a glass.'

'Let us have it here, then,' said the soldier, and when he had tasted one glass, he said, 'When wine is good, I like another glass,' and had another poured out for himself, and the rest followed his example.

'Hallo, comrades,' cried one of them to those who were in the stable, 'here is an old goody who has wine that is as old as herself; take a draught, it will warm your stomachs far better than our fire.'

The old woman carried her cask into the stable. One of the soldiers had seated himself on the saddled riding-horse, another held its bridle in his hand, and a third had laid hold of its tail. She poured out as much as they wanted until the spring ran dry. It was not long before the bridle fell from the hand of the one, and he fell down and began to snore; the other left hold of the tail, lay down, and snored still louder. The one who was sitting in the saddle did remain sitting, but bent his head almost down to the horse's neck, and slept, and blew with his mouth like the bellows of a forge. The soldiers outside had already been asleep for a long time, and were lying on the ground motionless, as if dead.

When the master-thief saw that he had succeeded, he gave the first a rope in his hand instead of the bridle, and the other who had been holding the tail, a wisp of straw, but what was he to do with the one who was sitting on the horse's back? He did not want to throw him down, for he might have awakened and have uttered a cry. He had a good idea; he unbuckled the girths of the saddle, tied a couple of ropes which were hanging to a ring on the wall fast to the saddle, and drew the sleeping rider up into the air on it. Then he twisted the rope round the posts, and made it fast. He soon unloosed the horse from the chain, but if he had ridden over the stony pavement of the yard they would have heard the noise in the castle. So he wrapped the horse's hoofs in old rags, led him carefully out, leapt upon him, and galloped off.

When day broke, the master galloped to the castle on the stolen horse. The count had just got up, and was looking out of the window. 'Good morning, Sir Count,' he cried to him, 'here is the horse, which I have got safely out of the stable! Just look, how beautifully your soldiers are lying there sleeping; and if you will but

go into the stable, you will see how comfortable your watchers have made it for themselves.'

The count could not help laughing; then he said, 'For once you have succeeded, but things won't go so well the second time, and I warn you that if you come before me as a thief, I will handle you as I would a thief.'

When the countess went to bed that night, she closed her hand with the wedding-ring tightly together, and the count said, 'All the doors are locked and bolted; I will keep awake and wait for the thief, but if he gets in by the window, I will shoot him.'

The master-thief, however, went in the dark to the gallows, cut a poor sinner who was hanging there down from the halter, and carried him on his back to the castle. Then he set a ladder up to the bedroom, put the dead body on his shoulders, and began to climb up. When he had got so high that the head of the dead man showed at the window, the count, who was watching in his bed, fired a pistol at him, and immediately the master let the poor sinner fall down and hid himself in one corner.

The night was sufficiently lighted by the moon for the master to see distinctly how the count got out of the window on to the ladder, came down, carried the dead body into the garden, and began to dig a hole in which to lay it. 'Now,' thought the thief, 'the favourable moment has come,' and he stole nimbly out of his corner, and climbed up the ladder straight into the countess's bedroom.

'Dear wife,' he began in the count's voice, 'the thief is dead, but, after all, he is my godson, and has been more of a scapegrace than a villain. I will not put him to open shame; besides, I am sorry for the parents. I will bury him myself before daybreak in the garden, that the thing may not be known, so give me the sheet. I will wrap up the body in it, and bury him as a dog buries things by scratching.' The countess gave him the sheet.

'I tell you what,' continued the thief, 'I have a fit of magnanimity on me; give me the ring, too—the unhappy man risked his life for it, so he may take it with him into his grave.' She would not gainsay the count, and although she did it unwillingly she drew the ring from her finger and gave it to him.

The thief made off with both these things and reached home safely before the count in the garden had finished his work of burying.

What a long face the count did pull when the master came next morning, and brought him the sheet and the ring. 'Are you a wizard?' said he. 'Who has fetched you out of the grave in which I myself laid you, and brought you to life again?'

'You did not bury me,' said the thief, 'but the poor sinner on the gallows,' and he told him exactly how everything had happened. And the count was forced to own to him that he was a clever, crafty thief.

'But you have not reached the end yet,' he added, 'you have still to perform the third task, and if you do not succeed in that, all this is of no use.' The master smiled and returned no answer.

When night had fallen he went with a long sack on his back, a bundle under his arms, and a lantern in his hand, to the village church. In the sack he had some crabs, and in the bundle, short wax candles. He sat down in the churchyard, took out a crab, and stuck a wax candle on his back. Then he lighted the little light, put the crab on the ground, and let it creep about. He took a second out of the sack, and treated it in the same way, and so on until the last was out of the sack. Hereupon he put on a long black garment that looked like a monk's cowl, and stuck a grey beard on his chin. When at last he was quite unrecognisable, he took the sack in which the crabs had been, went into the church, and ascended the pulpit.

The clock in the tower was just striking twelve; when the last stroke had sounded, he cried with a loud and piercing voice, 'Hearken, sinful men, the end of all things has come! The last day is at hand! Hearken! Hearken! Whosoever wishes to go to heaven with me must creep into the sack. I am Peter, who opens and shuts the gates of heaven. Behold how the dead outside there in the churchyard are wandering about collecting their bones. Come, come, and creep into the sack; the world is about to be destroyed!'

The cry echoed through the whole village. The parson and the clerk, who lived nearest to the church, heard it first, and when they saw the lights which were moving about the churchyard, they observed that something unusual was going on, and went into the church. They listened to the sermon for a while, and then the clerk nudged the parson, and said, 'It would not be amiss if we were to use the opportunity together, and before the dawning of the last day, find an easy way of getting to heaven.'

'To tell the truth,' answered the parson, 'that is what I myself have been thinking, so if you are inclined, we will set out on our way.'

'Yes,' answered the clerk, 'but you, the parson, have the precedence; I will follow.'

So the parson went first, and ascended the pulpit where the master opened his sack. The parson crept in first, and then the clerk. The master immediately tied up the sack tightly, seized it by the middle, and dragged it down the pulpit-steps, and whenever the heads of the two fools bumped against the steps, he cried, 'We are going over the mountains.' Then he drew them through the village in the same way, and when they were passing through puddles, he cried, 'Now we are going through wet clouds,' and when at last he was dragging them up the steps of the castle, he cried, 'Now we are on the steps of heaven, and will soon be in the outer court.' When he had got to the top, he pushed the sack into the pigeon-house, and when the pigeons fluttered about, he said, 'Hark how glad the angels are, and how they are flapping their wings!' Then he bolted the door upon them and went away.

Next morning he went to the count, and told him that he had performed the third task also, and had carried the parson and clerk out of the church.

'Where have you left them?' asked the lord.

'They are lying upstairs in a sack in the pigeon-house, and imagine that they are in heaven.'

The count went up himself, and convinced himself that the master had told the truth. When he had delivered the parson and clerk from their captivity, he said, 'You are an arch-thief, and have won your wager. For once you escape with a whole skin, but see that you leave my land, for if ever you set foot on it again, you may count on your elevation to the gallows.'

The arch-thief took leave of his parents, once more went forth into the wide world, and no one has ever heard of him since.

THE NIX OF THE MILL-POND

There was once upon a time a miller who lived with his wife in great contentment. They had money and land, and their prosperity increased year by year more and more. But ill-luck comes like a thief in the night; as their wealth had increased, so did it again decrease, year by year, and at last the miller could hardly call the mill in which he lived his own. He was in great distress, and when he lay down after his day's work, found no rest, but tossed about in his bed, full of care.

One morning he rose before daybreak and went out into the open air, thinking that perhaps there his heart might become lighter. As he was stepping over the mill-dam the first sunbeam was just breaking forth, and he heard a rippling sound in the pond. He turned round and perceived a beautiful woman rising slowly out of the water. Her long hair, which she was holding off her shoulders with her soft hands, fell down on both sides and covered her white body. He soon saw that she was the nix of the mill-pond, and in his fright did not know whether he should run away or stay where he was. But the nix made her sweet voice heard, called him by his name, and asked him why he was so sad? The miller was at first struck dumb, but when he heard her speak so kindly he took heart and told her how he had formerly lived in wealth and happiness, but that now he was so poor that he did not know what to do.

'Be easy,' answered the nix, 'I will make you richer and happier than you have ever been before, only you must promise to give me the young thing which has just been born in your house.'

'What else can that be,' thought the miller, 'but a young puppy or kitten?' and he promised what she desired.

The nix descended into the water again, and he hurried back to his mill, consoled and in good spirits. He had not yet reached it, when the maid-servant came out of the house and cried to him to rejoice, for his wife had given birth to a little boy. The miller stood as if struck by lightning; he saw very well that the cunning nix had been aware of it and had cheated him. Hanging his head, he went up to his wife's bedside, and when she said, 'Why do you not rejoice over the fine boy?' he told her what had befallen him, and what kind of a promise he had given to the nix.

'Of what use to me are riches and prosperity?' he added, 'if I am to lose my child; but what can I do?'

Even the relations, who had come thither to wish them joy, did not know what to say.

In the meantime, prosperity again returned to the miller's house. All that he

undertook succeeded; it was as if presses and coffers filled themselves of their own accord, and as if money multiplied nightly in the cupboards. It was not long before his wealth was greater than it had ever been before. But he could not rejoice over it untroubled; the bargain which he had made with the nix tormented his soul. Whenever he passed the mill-pond, he feared she might ascend and remind him of his debt. He never let the boy himself go near the water. 'Beware,' he said to him, 'if thou dost but touch the water, a hand will rise, seize thee, and draw thee down.'

But as year after year went by and the nix did not show herself again, the miller began to feel at ease. The boy grew up to be a youth and was apprenticed to a huntsman. When he had learnt everything, and had become an excellent huntsman, the lord of the village took him into his service. In the village lived a beautiful and true-hearted maiden, who pleased the huntsman, and when his master perceived that, he gave him a little house; the two were married, lived peacefully and happily, and loved each other with all their hearts.

One day the huntsman was chasing a roe; and when the animal turned aside from the forest into the open country, he pursued it and at last shot it. He did not notice that he was now in the neighbourhood of the dangerous mill-pond, and went, after he had disembowelled the roe, to the water, in order to wash his blood-stained hands. Scarcely, however, had he dipped them in than the nix ascended, smilingly wound her dripping arms around him, and drew him quickly down under the waves, which closed over him.

When it was evening and the huntsman did not return home, his wife became alarmed. She went out to seek him, and as he had often told her that he had to be on his guard against the snares of the nix and dared not venture into the neighbourhood of the mill-pond, she already suspected what had happened. She hastened to the water, and when she found his hunting pouch lying on the shore, she could no longer have any doubt of the misfortune. Lamenting her sorrow and wringing her hands, she called on her beloved by name, but in vain. She hurried across to the other side of the pond and called him anew; she reviled the nix with harsh words, but no answer followed. The surface of the water remained calm; only the crescent moon stared steadily back at her. The poor woman did not leave the pond. With hasty steps she paced round and round it, without resting a moment, sometimes in silence, sometimes uttering a loud cry, sometimes softly sobbing.

At last her strength came to an end, and she sank down to the ground and fell into a heavy sleep. Presently a dream took possession of her. She was anxiously climbing upwards between great masses of rock; thorns and briars caught her feet, the rain beat in her face, and the wind tossed her long hair about. When she reached the summit, quite a different sight presented itself to her; the sky was blue, the air soft, and the ground sloped gently downwards, and on a green meadow, gay with flowers of every colour, stood a pretty cottage. She went up to it and opened the door; there sat an old woman with white hair, who beckoned to her kindly.

At that very moment the poor woman awoke. Day had already dawned, and she at once resolved to act in accordance with her dream. She laboriously climbed the mountain; everything was exactly as she had seen it in the night. The old woman received her kindly, and pointed out a chair on which she might sit. 'You must have met with a misfortune,' she said, 'since you have sought out my lonely cottage.'

With tears, the woman related what had befallen her.

'Be comforted,' said the old woman, 'I will help you. Here is a golden comb for you. Tarry till the full moon has risen, then go to the mill-pond, seat yourself on the shore, and comb your long black hair with this comb. When you have done, lay it down on the bank, and you will see what will happen.'

The woman returned home, but the time till the full moon came passed slowly. At last the shining disc appeared in the heavens. Then she went out to the mill-pond, sat down and combed her long black hair with the golden comb, and when she had finished, she laid the comb down at the water's edge. It was not long before there was a movement in the depths; a wave rose, rolled to the shore, and bore the comb away with it. In not more than the time necessary for the comb to sink to the bottom, the surface of the water parted and the head of the huntsman arose. He did not speak, but looked at his wife with sorrowful glances. At the same instant, a second wave came rushing up and covered the man's head. All had vanished; the mill-pond lay peaceful as before, and nothing but the face of the full moon shone on it.

Full of sorrow, the woman went back, but again the dream showed her the cottage of the old woman. Next morning she again set out and complained of her woes to the wise woman. The old woman gave her a golden flute, and said, 'Tarry till the full moon comes again, then take this flute; play a beautiful air on it, and when you have finished, lay it on the sand; then you will see what will happen.'

The wife did as the old woman told her. No sooner was the flute lying on the sand than there was a stirring in the depths, and a wave rushed up and bore the flute away with it. Immediately afterwards, the water parted, and not only the head of the man, but half of his body also arose. He stretched out his arms longingly towards her, but a second wave came up, covered him, and drew him down again. 'Alas, what does it profit me?' said the unhappy woman, 'that I should see my beloved, only to lose him again!'

Despair filled her heart anew, but the dream led her a third time to the house of the old woman. She set out, and the wise woman gave her a golden spinning-wheel, consoled her and said, 'All is not yet fulfilled; tarry until the time of the full moon, then take the spinning wheel, seat yourself on the shore, and spin the spool full, and when you have done that, place the spinning-wheel near the water, and you will see what will happen.'

The woman obeyed all she said exactly. As soon as the full moon showed itself, she carried the spinning-wheel to the shore, and spun industriously until the flax came to an end and the spool was quite filled with the threads. No sooner was the wheel standing on the shore than there was a more violent movement than before in the depths of the pond, and a mighty wave rushed up and bore the wheel away with it. Immediately the head and the whole body of the man rose into the air, in a water-spout. He quickly sprang to the shore, caught his wife by the hand and fled. But they had scarcely gone a very little distance, when the whole pond rose with a frightful roar and streamed out over the open country. The fugitives already saw death before their eyes, when the woman in her terror implored the help of the old woman, and in an instant they were transformed, she into a toad, he into a frog.

The flood which had overtaken them could not destroy them, but it tore them apart and carried them far away. When the water had dispersed and they both touched dry land again, they regained their human form, but neither knew where the other was; they found themselves among strange people, who did not know their native land. High mountains and deep valleys lay between them. In order to keep themselves alive, they were both obliged to tend sheep.

For many long years they drove their flocks through field and forest and were full of sorrow and longing. When spring had once more broken forth on the earth, they both went out one day with their flocks, and as chance would have it, they drew near each other. They met in a valley but did not recognise each other; yet they rejoiced that they were no longer so lonely. Henceforth they each day drove their flocks to the same place; they did not speak much, but they felt comforted.

One evening when the full moon was shining in the sky and the sheep were already at rest, the shepherd pulled the flute out of his pocket and played on it a beautiful but sorrowful air. When he had finished he saw that the shepherdess was weeping bitterly. 'Why are you weeping?' he asked.

'Alas,' answered she, 'thus shone the full moon when I played this air on the flute for the last time, and the head of my beloved rose out of the water.'

He looked at her, and it seemed as if a veil fell from his eyes and he recognised his dear wife, and when she looked at him, and the moon shone in his face, she knew him also. They embraced and kissed each other, and no one need ask if they were happy.

There was once a King whose castle was surrounded by a forest full of game. One day he sent a huntsman out to shoot a deer, but he never came back.

'Perhaps an accident has happened to him,' said the King.

Next day he sent out two more huntsmen to look for him, but they did not return either.

On the third day he sent for all his huntsmen, and said to them, 'Search the whole forest without ceasing, until you have found all three.'

But not a single man of all these, or one of the pack of hounds they took with them, ever came back. From this time forth no one would venture into the forest; so there it lay, wrapped in silence and solitude, with only an occasional eagle or hawk circling over it.

This continued for several years, and then one day a strange huntsman sought an audience of the King, and offered to penetrate into the dangerous wood. The King, however, would not give him permission, and said, 'It's not safe, and I am afraid if you go in that you will never come out again, any more than all the others.'

The huntsman answered, 'Sire, I will take the risk upon myself. I do not know fear.'

So the huntsman went into the wood with his dog. Before long the dog put up some game and wanted to chase it; but hardly had he taken a few steps when he came to a deep pool, and could go no further. A naked arm appeared out of the water, seized him, and drew him down.

When the huntsman saw this, he went back and fetched three men with pails to empty the pool. When they got to the bottom they found a wild man, whose body was as brown as rusty iron, and whose hair hung down over his face to his knees. They bound him with cords, and carried him away to the castle. There was great excitement over the wild man, whose name was Iron Hans, and the King had an iron cage made for him in the courtyard. He forbade anyone to open the door on pain of death, and the Queen had to keep the key.

After this, anybody could walk in the forest with safety.

The King had a little son eight years old, and one day he was playing in the courtyard. In his play his golden ball fell into the cage. The boy ran up, and said, 'Give me back my ball.'

'Not until you have opened the door,' said the wild man.

'No; I can't do that,' said the boy, 'my father has forbidden it,' and then he ran away.

Next day he came again, and asked for his ball. The man said, 'Open my door,' but he would not.

On the third day the King went out hunting, and the boy came again, and said, 'Even if I would, I could not open the door. I have not got the key.'

Then the wild man said, 'It is lying under your mother's pillow. You can easily get it.'

The boy, who was very anxious to have his ball back, threw his scruples to the winds, and fetched the key. The door was very stiff, and he pinched his fingers in opening it. As soon as it was open the wild man came out, gave the boy his ball, and hurried away. The boy was now very frightened, and cried out, 'Oh, wild man, don't go away, or I shall be beaten!'

The wild man turned back, picked up the boy, put him on his shoulder, and walked hurriedly off into the wood.

When the King came home he saw at once the cage was empty, and asked the Queen how it had come about. She knew nothing about it, and went to look for the key, which was of course gone. They called the boy, but there was no answer. The King sent people out into the fields to look for him, but all in vain; he was gone. The King easily guessed what had happened, and great grief fell on the royal household.

When the wild man got back into the depths of the dark forest he took the boy down off his shoulder and said, 'You will never see your father and mother again; but I will keep you here with me, because you had pity on me and set me free. If you do as you are told, you will be well treated. I have treasures and gold enough and to spare, more than anybody in the world.'

He made a bed of moss for the boy, on which he went to sleep. Next morning the man led him to a spring and said, 'You see this golden well is bright and clear as crystal? You must sit by it, and take care that nothing falls into it, or it will be contaminated. I shall come every evening to see if you have obeyed my orders.'

The boy sat down on the edge of the spring to watch it; sometimes he would see a gold fish or a golden snake darting through it, and he guarded it well, so that nothing should fall into it. One day as he was sitting like this his finger pained him so much that involuntarily he dipped it into the water. He drew it out very quickly, but saw that it was gilded, and although he tried hard to clean it, it remained golden. In the evening Iron Hans came back, looked at the boy, and said, 'What has happened to the well today?'

'Nothing, nothing!' he answered, keeping his finger behind his back so that Iron Hans should not see it.

But he said, 'You have dipped your finger into the water. It does not matter this time, but take care that nothing of the kind occurs again.'

Early next morning the boy took his seat by the spring again to watch. His finger still hurt very much, and he put his hand up above his head; but, unfortunately, in so doing he brushed a hair into the well. He quickly took it out, but it was already gilded. When Iron Hans came in the evening, he knew very well what had happened.

'You have let a hair fall into the well,' he said. 'I will overlook it once more, but if it happens for the third time the well will be polluted, and you can no longer stay with me.'

On the third day the boy again sat by the well; but he took good care not to move a finger, however much it might hurt. The time seemed very long to him as he looked at his face reflected in the water. As he bent over further and further to look into his eyes, his long hair fell over his shoulder right into the water. He started up at once, but not before his whole head of hair had become golden, and glittered like the sun. You may imagine how frightened the poor boy was. He took his pocket-handkerchief and tied it over his head, so that Iron Hans should not see it. But he knew all about it before he came, and at once said, 'Take that handkerchief off your head,' and then all the golden hair tumbled out. All the poor boy's excuses were no good. 'You have not stood the test, and you can no longer stay here. You must go out into the world, and there you will learn the meaning of poverty. But as your heart is not bad, and as I wish you well, I will grant you one thing. When you are in great need, go to the forest and cry "Iron Hans", and I will come and help you. My power is great, greater than you think, and I have gold and silver in abundance.'

So the King's son left the forest, and wandered over trodden and untrodden paths till he reached a great city. He tried to get work, but he could not find any; besides, he knew no trade by which to make a living. At last he went to the castle and asked if they would employ him. The courtiers did not know what use they could make of him, but they were taken with his appearance, and said he might stay. At last the cook took him into his service, and said he might carry wood and water for him and sweep up the ashes.

One day, as there was no one else at hand, the cook ordered him to carry the food up to the royal table. As he did not want his golden hair to be seen, he kept his cap on. Nothing of the sort had ever happened in the presence of the King before, and he said, 'When you come into the royal presence, you must take your cap off.'

'Alas, Sire,' he said, 'I cannot take it off, because I have a bad wound on my head.'

Then the King ordered the cook to be called, and asked how he could take such a boy into his service, and ordered him to be sent away at once. But the cook was sorry for him, and exchanged him with the gardener's boy.

Now the boy had to dig and hoe, plant and water, in every kind of weather.

One day in the summer when he was working alone in the garden it was very hot, and he took off his cap for the fresh air to cool his head. When the sun shone on his hair it glittered so that the beams penetrated right into the Princess's bedroom, and she sprang up to see what it was. She discovered the youth, and called to him, 'Bring me a nosegay, young man.'

He hurriedly put on his cap, picked a lot of wild flowers, and tied them up. On his way up to the Princess, the gardener met him, and said, 'How can you take such poor flowers to the Princess? Quickly cut another bouquet, and mind they are the choicest and rarest flowers.'

'Oh, no,' said the youth. 'The wild flowers have a sweeter scent, and will please her better.'

As soon as he went into the room the Princess said, 'Take off your cap; it is not proper for you to wear it before me.'

He answered again, 'I may not take it off, because I have a wound on my head.'

But she took hold of the cap, and pulled it off, and all his golden hair tumbled over his shoulders in a shower. It was quite a sight. He tried to get away, but she took hold of his arm and gave him a handful of ducats. He took them, but he cared nothing for the gold and gave it to the gardener for his children to play with.

Next day the Princess again called him to bring her a bunch of wild flowers, and when he brought it she immediately clutched at his cap to pull it off; but he held it on with both hands. Again she gave him a handful of ducats, but he would not keep them, and gave them to the gardener's children. The third day the same thing happened, but she could not take off his cap, and he would not keep the gold.

Not long after this the kingdom was invaded. The King assembled his warriors. He did not know whether they would be able to conquer his enemies or not, as they were very powerful and had a mighty army. Then the gardener's assistant said, 'I have been brought up to fight; give me a horse, and I will go too.'

The others laughed and said, 'When we are gone, find one for yourself. We will leave one behind in the stable for you.'

When they were gone, he went and got the horse out; it was lame in one leg, and hobbled along, humpety-hump, humpety-hump. Nevertheless, he mounted it and rode away to the dark forest. When he came to the edge of it, he called three times, 'Iron Hans' as loud as he could, till the trees resounded with it.

The wild man appeared immediately, and said, 'What do you want?'

'I want a strong horse to go to the war.'

'You shall have it, and more besides.'

The wild man went back into the wood, and before long a groom came out, leading a fiery charger with snorting nostrils. Behind him followed a great body of warriors all in armour, and their swords gleaming in the sun. The youth handed over his three-legged steed to the groom, mounted the other, and rode away at the head of the troop.

When he approached the battle-field a great many of the King's men had already fallen, and before long the rest must have given in. Then the youth, at the head of his iron troop, charged, and bore down the enemy like a mighty wind, smiting everything in the way. They tried to fly, but the youth fell upon them, and did not stop while one remained alive.

Instead of joining the King, he led his troop straight back to the wood and called Iron Hans again.

'What do you want?' asked the wild man.

'Take back your charger and your troop, and give me back my three-legged steed.'

His request was granted, and he rode his three-legged steed home.

When the King returned to the castle his daughter met him and congratulated him on his victory.

'It was not I who won it,' he said; 'but a strange knight, who came to my assistance with his troop.' His daughter asked who the strange knight was, but the King did not know, and said, 'He pursued the enemy, and I have not seen him since.'

She asked the gardener about his assistant, but he laughed and said, 'He has just come home on his three-legged horse, and the others made fun of him and said, "Here comes our hobbler back again," and asked which hedge he had been sleeping under. He answered, "I did my best, and without me things would have gone badly." Then they laughed at him more than ever.'

The King said to his daughter, 'I will give a great feast lasting three days, and you shall throw a golden apple. Perhaps the unknown knight will come among the others to try and catch it.'

When notice was given of the feast, the youth went to the wood and called Iron Hans.

'What do you want?' he asked.

'I want to secure the King's golden apple,' he said.

'It is as good as yours already,' answered Iron Hans. 'You shall have a tawny suit, and ride a proud chestnut.'

When the day arrived the youth took his place among the other knights, but no one knew him. The Princess stepped forward and threw the apple among the knights, and he was the only one who could catch it. As soon as he had it he rode away.

On the second day Iron Hans fitted him out as a white knight, riding a gallant grey. Again he caught the apple; but he did not stay a minute, and, as before, hurried away.

The King now grew angry, and said, 'This must not be; he must come before me and give me his name.'

He gave an order that if the knight made off again he was to be pursued and brought back.

On the third day the youth received from Iron Hans a black outfit, and a fiery black charger.

Again he caught the apple; but as he was riding off with it, the King's people chased him, and one came so near that he wounded him in the leg. Still he escaped, but his horse galloped so fast that his helmet fell off, and they all saw that he had golden hair. So they rode back, and told the King what they had seen.

Next day the Princess asked the gardener about his assistant.

'He is working in the garden. The queer fellow went to the feast, and he only came back last night. He has shown my children three golden apples which he won.'

The King ordered him to be brought before him. When he appeared he still wore his cap. But the Princess went up to him and took it off; then all his golden hair fell over his shoulders, and it was so beautiful that they were all amazed by it.

'Are you the knight who came to the feast every day in a different colour and caught the three golden apples?' asked the King.

'Yes,' he answered, 'and here are the apples,' bringing them out of his pocket, and giving them to the King. 'If you want further proof, here is the wound in my leg given me by your people when they pursued me. But I am also the knight who helped you to conquer the enemy.'

'If you can do such deeds you are no gardener's boy. Tell me who is your father?'

'My father is a powerful King, and I have plenty of gold—as much as I ever want.'

'I see very well,' said the King, 'that we owe you many thanks. Can I do anything to please you?'

'Yes,' he answered; 'indeed, you can. Give me your daughter to be my wife!'

The maiden laughed, and said, 'He does not beat about the bush; but I saw long ago that he was no gardener's boy.'

Then she went up to him and kissed him.

His father and mother came to the wedding, and they were full of joy, for they had long given up all hope of ever seeing their dear son again. As they were all sitting at the wedding feast, the music suddenly stopped, the doors flew open, and a proud King walked in at the head of a great following. He went up to the bridegroom, embraced him, and said, 'I am Iron Hans, who was bewitched and changed into a wild man; but you have broken the spell and set me free. All the treasure that I have is now your own.'

GODFATHER DEATH

A poor man had twelve children and was forced to work night and day to give them even bread. When, therefore, the thirteenth came into the world, he knew not what to do in his trouble, but ran out into the great highway, and resolved to ask the first person he met to be godfather. The first to meet him was the good God who already knew what filled his heart, and said to him, 'Poor man, I pity thee. I will hold thy child at its christening, and will take charge of it and make it happy on earth.'

The man said, 'Who art thou?'

'I am God.'

'Then I do not desire to have thee for a godfather,' said the man; 'thou givest to the rich, and leavest the poor to hunger.' Thus spoke the man, for he did not know how wisely God apportions riches and poverty. He turned, therefore, away from the Lord, and went farther.

Then the Devil came to him, and said, 'What seekest thou? If thou wilt take me as a godfather for thy child, I will give him gold in plenty, and all the joys of the world as well.'

The man asked, 'Who art thou?'

'I am the Devil.'

'Then I do not desire to have thee for godfather,' said the man; 'thou deceivest men and leadest them astray.'

He went onwards, and then came Death striding up to him with withered legs, and said, 'Take me as godfather.'

The man asked, 'Who art thou?'

'I am Death, and I make all equal.'

Then said the man, 'Thou art the right one; thou takest the rich as well as the poor, without distinction; thou shalt be godfather.'

Death answered, 'I will make thy child rich and famous, for he who has me for a friend can lack nothing.'

The man said, 'Next Sunday is the christening; be there at the right time.'

Death appeared as he had promised, and stood godfather quite in the usual way.

When the boy had grown up, his godfather one day appeared and bade him go with him. He led him forth into a forest, and showed him a herb which grew there, and said, 'Now shalt thou receive thy godfather's present. I will make thee a celebrated physician. When thou art called to a patient, I will always appear to thee. If I stand by the head of the sick man, thou mayst say with confidence that thou wilt make him well again, and if thou givest him of this herb he will recover; but if I stand by the patient's feet, he is mine, and thou must say that all remedies are in vain, and that no physician in the world could save him. But beware of using the herb against my will, or it will fare ill with thee.'

It was not long before the youth was the most famous physician in the whole world. 'He had only to look at the patient and he knew his condition at once, and if he would recover, or must needs die.' So they said of him, and from far and wide people came to him, sent for him when they had anyone ill, and gave him so much money that he soon became a rich man.

Now it so befell that the King became ill, and the physician was summoned, and was to say if recovery were possible. But when he came to the bed, Death was standing by the feet of the sick man, and the herb did not grow which could save him. 'If I could but cheat Death for once,' thought the physician; 'he is sure to take it ill if I do, but, as I am his godson, he will shut one eye; I will risk it.' He therefore took up the sick man and laid him the other way, so that now Death was standing by his head. Then he gave the King some of the herb, and he recovered and grew healthy again.

But Death came to the physician, looking very black and angry, threatened him with his finger, and said, 'Thou hast overreached me; this time I will pardon it, as thou art my godson. But if thou venturest it again, it will cost thee thy neck, for I will take thee thyself away with me.'

Soon afterwards the King's daughter fell into a severe illness. She was his only child, and he wept day and night, so that he began to lose the sight of his eyes, and he caused it to be made known that whosoever rescued her from death should be her husband and inherit the crown. When the physician came to the sick girl's bed, he saw Death by her feet. He ought to have remembered the warning given by his godfather, but he was so infatuated by the great beauty of the King's daughter, and the happiness of becoming her husband, that he flung all thought to the winds. He did not see that Death was casting angry glances on him, that he was raising his hand in the air and threatening him with his withered fist. He raised up the sick girl, and placed her head where her feet had lain. Then he gave her some of the herb, and instantly her cheeks flushed red, and life stirred afresh in her.

When Death saw that for a second time he was defrauded of his own property, he walked up to the physician with long strides, and said, 'All is over with thee, and now the lot falls on thee,' and seized him so firmly with his ice-cold hand that he could not resist, and led him into a cave below the earth. There he saw how thousands and thousands of candles were burning in countless rows, some large, others half-sized, others small. Every instant some were extinguished, and others again burnt up, so that the flames seemed to leap hither and thither in perpetual change. 'See,' said Death, 'these are the lights of men's lives. The large ones belong to children, the half-sized ones to married people in their prime, the little ones belong to old folk; but children and young folks likewise have often only a tiny candle.'

'Show me the light of my life,' said the physician, and he thought that it would still be very tall. Death pointed to a little end which was just threatening to go out, and said, 'Behold, it is there.'

'Ah, dear godfather,' said the horrified physician, 'light a new one for me, do it for love of me, that I may enjoy my life, be King, and the husband of the King's beautiful daughter.'

'I cannot,' answered Death. 'One must go out before a new one is lighted.'

'Then place the old one on a new one, that will go on burning at once when the old one has come to an end,' pleaded the physician.

Death behaved as if he were going to fulfil his wish, and took hold of a tall new candle; but as he desired to revenge himself he purposely made a mistake in fixing it, and the little piece fell down and was extinguished. Immediately the physician fell on the ground, and now he himself was in the hands of Death.

Lhere was once a young huntsman who went into the forest to lie in wait. He had a fresh and joyous heart, and as he was going thither, whistling upon a leaf, an ugly old crone came up who spoke to him and said, 'Good-day, dear huntsman, truly you are merry and contented, but I am suffering from hunger and thirst; do give me an alms.'

The huntsman had compassion on the poor old creature, felt in his pocket, and gave her what he could afford. He was then about to go further, but the old woman stopped him and said, 'Listen, dear huntsman, to what I tell you; I will make you a present in return for your kindness. Go on your way now, but in a little while you will come to a tree whereon nine birds are sitting which have a cloak in their claws, and are plucking at it. Take your gun and shoot into the midst of them; they will let the cloak fall down to you, but one of the birds will be hurt and will drop down dead. Carry away the cloak. It is a wishing-cloak; when you throw it over your shoulders you only have to wish to be in a certain place and you will be there in the twinkling of an eye. Take out the heart of the dead bird and swallow it whole, and every morning early, when you get up, you will find a gold piece under your pillow.'

The huntsman thanked the wise woman, and thought to himself, 'Those are fine things that she has promised me, if all does but come true.' And verily, when he had walked about a hundred paces, he heard in the branches above him such a screaming and twittering that he looked up and saw there a crowd of birds who were tearing a piece of cloth about with their beaks and claws, and tugging and fighting as if each wanted to have it all to himself. 'Well,' said the huntsman, 'this is wonderful; it has really come to pass just as the old wife foretold!' and he took the gun from his shoulder, aimed, and fired right into the midst of them, so that the feathers flew about. The birds instantly took to flight with loud outcries, but one dropped down dead, and the cloak fell at the same time. Then the huntsman did as the old woman had directed, cut open the bird, sought the heart, swallowed it down, and took the cloak home with him.

Next morning when he awoke the promise occurred to him, and he wished to see if it also had been fulfilled. When he lifted up the pillow, the gold piece shone in his eyes, and next day he found another, and so it went on, every time he got up. He gathered together a heap of gold, but at last he thought, 'Of what use is all my gold to me if I stay at home? I will go forth and see the world.'

He then took leave of his parents, buckled on his huntsman's pouch and gun, and went out into the world.

It came to pass that one day he travelled through a dense forest, and when he came to the end of it, in the plain before him stood a fine castle. An old woman was standing with a wonderfully beautiful maiden, looking out of one of the windows.

The old woman, however, was a witch, and said to the maiden, 'There comes one out of the forest who has a wonderful treasure in his body; we must filch it from him, my dear daughter, it is more suitable for us than for him. He has a bird's heart about him, by means of which a gold piece lies every morning under his pillow.' She told her what she was to do to get it, and what part she had to play, and finally threatened her and said with angry eyes, 'And if you do not attend to what I say, it will be the worse for you.'

Now when the huntsman came nearer he descried the maiden, and said to himself, 'I have travelled about for such a long time, I will take a rest for once, and enter that beautiful castle. I have certainly money enough.' Nevertheless, the real reason was that he had caught sight of the beautiful girl.

He entered the house, and was well received and courteously entertained. Before long he was so much in love with the young witch that he no longer thought of anything else, and only saw things as she saw them, and did what she desired.

The old woman then said, 'Now we must have the bird's heart; he will never miss it.' She prepared a drink, and when it was ready poured it into a cup and gave it to the maiden, who was to present it to the huntsman. She did so, saying, 'Now, my dearest, drink to me.'

So he took the cup, and when he had swallowed the draught, he brought up the heart of the bird. The girl had to take it away secretly and swallow it herself, for the old woman would have it so. Thenceforward, he found no more gold under his pillow, but it lay instead under that of the maiden, from whence the old woman fetched it away every morning; but he was so much in love and so befooled, that he thought of nothing else but of passing his time with the girl.

Then the old witch said, 'We have the bird's heart, but we must also take the wishing-cloak away from him.'

The girl answered, 'We will leave him that; he has lost his wealth.'

The old woman was angry and said, 'Such a mantle is a wonderful thing, and is seldom to be found in this world. I must and will have it!' She gave the girl several blows, and said that if she did not obey it should fare ill with her. So she did the old woman's bidding, placed herself at the window and looked on the distant country, as if she were very sorrowful.

The huntsman asked, 'Why dost thou stand there so sorrowfully?'

'Ah, my beloved,' was her answer, 'over yonder lies the Garnet Mountain, where the precious stones grow. I long for them so much that when I think of them I feel quite sad, but who can get them? Only the birds; they fly and can reach them, but a man, never.'

'Hast thou nothing else to complain of?' said the huntsman. 'I will soon remove that burden from thy heart.'

With that, he drew her under his mantle, wished himself on the Garnet Mountain, and in the twinkling of an eye they were sitting on it together. Precious stones were glistening on every side, so that it was a joy to see them, and together they gathered the finest and costliest of them. Now the old woman had, through her sorceries, contrived that the eyes of the huntsman should become heavy. He said to the maiden, 'We will sit down and rest awhile; I am so tired that I can no longer stand on my feet.' Then they sat down, and he laid his head in her lap and fell asleep. When he was asleep, she unfastened the mantle from his shoulders and wrapped herself in it, picked up the garnets and stones, and wished herself back at home with them.

But when the huntsman had had his sleep out and awoke, and perceived that his sweetheart had betrayed him and left him alone on the wild mountain, he said, 'Oh, what treachery there is in the world!' and sat down there in care and sorrow, not knowing what to do. But the mountain belonged to some wild and monstrous giants who dwelt thereon and lived their lives there, and he had not sat long before he saw three of them coming towards him, so he lay down as if he were sunk in a deep sleep.

Then the giants came up, and the first kicked him with his foot and said, 'What sort of an earth-worm is lying curled up here?'

The second said, 'Step upon him and kill him.'

But the third said, 'That would indeed be worth your while. Just let him live, he cannot remain here; and when he climbs higher, towards the summit of the mountain, the clouds will lay hold of him and bear him away.'

So saying, they passed by.

But the huntsman had paid heed to their words, and as soon as they were gone, he rose and climbed up to the summit of the mountain, and when he had sat there a while a cloud floated towards him, caught him up, carried him away, and travelled about for a long time in the heavens. Then it sank lower, and let itself down on a great cabbage-garden, girt round by walls, so that he came softly to the ground on cabbages and vegetables.

Then the huntsman looked about him and said, 'If I had but something to eat! I am so hungry, and my hunger will increase in course of time; but I see here neither apples nor pears, nor any other sort of fruit—everywhere nothing but cabbages.' But at length he thought, 'At a pinch I can eat some of the leaves; they do not taste particuiarly good, but they will refresh me.' With that, he picked himself out a fine head of cabbage and ate it, but scarcely had he swallowed a couple of mouthfuls than he felt very strange and quite different.

Four legs grew on him, a large head and two thick ears, and he saw with horror that he was changed into an ass. Still, as his hunger increased every minute, and as the juicy leaves were suitable to his present nature, he went on eating with great zest. At last he arrived at a different kind of cabbage, but as soon as he had swallowed it he again felt a change, and reassumed his former shape.

Then the huntsman lay down and slept off his fatigue. When he awoke next morning, he broke off one head of the bad cabbages and another of the good ones, and thought to himself, 'This shall help me to get my own again and punish treachery.' Then he took the cabbages with him, climbed over the wall, and went forth to seek for the castle of his sweetheart. After wandering about for a couple of days he was lucky enough to find it again. He dyed his face brown, so that his own mother would not have known him, and begged for shelter: 'I am so tired,' said he, 'that I can go no further.'

The witch asked, 'Who are you, countryman, and what is your business?'

'I am a King's messenger, and was sent out to seek the most delicious salad that grows beneath the sun. I have even been so fortunate as to find it, and am carrying it about with me; but the heat of the sun is so intense that the delicate cabbage threatens to wither, and I do not know if I can carry it any further.'

When the old woman heard of the exquisite salad, she was greedy, and said, 'Dear countryman, let me just taste this wonderful salad.'

'Why not?' answered he, 'I have brought two heads with me, and will give you one of them,' and he opened his pouch and handed her the bad cabbage.

The witch suspected nothing amiss, and her mouth watered so for this new dish that she herself went into the kitchen and dressed it. When it was prepared she could not wait until it was set on the table, but took a couple of leaves at once; but hardly had she swallowed them than she was deprived of her human shape, and she ran out into the courtyard in the form of an ass.

Presently the maidservant entered the kitchen, saw the salad standing there ready prepared, and was about to carry it up; but on the way, according to habit, she was seized by the desire to taste, and she ate a couple of leaves. Instantly, the magic power showed itself, and she likewise became an ass and ran out to the old woman, and the dish of salad fell to the ground.

Meantime the messenger sat beside the beautiful girl, and as no one came with the salad and she also was longing for it, she said, 'I don't know what has become of the salad.'

The huntsman thought, 'The salad must have already taken effect,' and said, 'I will go to the kitchen and enquire about it.' As he went down he saw the two asses running about in the courtyard; the salad, however, was lying on the ground.

'All right,' said he, 'the two have taken their portion,' and he picked up the other leaves, laid them on the dish, and carried them to the maiden. 'I bring you the delicate food myself,' said he, 'in order that you may not have to wait longer.'

Then she ate of it, and was, like the others, immediately deprived of her human form, and ran out into the courtyard in the shape of an ass.

After the huntsman had washed his face, so that the transformed ones could recognise him, he went down into the courtyard and said, 'Now you shall receive the wages of your treachery,' and bound them together, all three with one rope, and drove them along until he came to a mill. He knocked at the window; the miller put out his head, and asked what he wanted.

'I have three unmanageable beasts,' answered he, 'which I don't want to keep any longer. Will you take them in and give them food and stable room, and manage them as I tell you, and I will pay what you ask.'

The miller said, 'Why not? but how am I to manage them?'

The huntsman then said that he was to give three beatings and one meal daily to the old donkey, and that was the witch; one beating and three meals to the younger one, which was the servant-girl; and to the youngest, which was the maiden, no beatings and three meals, for he could not bring himself to have the maiden beaten. After that he went back into the castle and found therein everything he needed.

After a couple of days, the miller came and said he must inform him that the old ass which had received three beatings and only one meal daily was dead; 'the two others,' he continued, 'are certainly not dead, and are fed three times daily, but they are so sad that they cannot last much longer.'

The huntsman was moved to pity, put away his anger, and told the miller to drive them back again to him. And when they came, he gave them some of the good salad, so that they became human again.

The beautiful girl fell on her knees before him, and said, 'Ah, my beloved, forgive me for the evil I have done you; my mother drove me to it; it was done against my will, for I love you dearly. Your wishing-cloak hangs in a cupboard, and as for the bird's heart, I will take a vomiting potion.'

But he thought otherwise, and said, 'Keep it; it is all the same, for I will take thee for my true wife.'

So the wedding was celebrated, and they lived happily together until their death.

THE BREMEN TOWN-MUSICIANS

Once upon a time a man had an ass which for many years carried sacks to the mill without tiring. At last, however, its strength was worn out; it was no longer of any use for work. Accordingly, its master began to ponder as to how best to cut down its keep; but the ass, seeing there was mischief in the air, ran away and started on the road to Bremen. There he thought he could become a town-musician.

When he had been travelling a short time, he fell in with a hound, who was lying panting on the road as though he had run himself off his legs.

'Well, what are you panting so for, Growler?' said the ass.

'Ah,' said the hound, 'just because I am old, and every day I get weaker, and also because I can no longer keep up with the pack, my master wanted to kill me, so I took my departure. But now, how am I to earn my bread? '

'Do you know what,' said the ass, 'I am going to Bremen, and shall there become a town-musician; come with me and take your part in the music. I shall play the lute, and you shall beat the kettle-drum.'

The hound agreed, and they went on.

A short time after they came upon a cat, sitting in the road, with a face like three rainy days.

'Well, what has been crossing you, Whiskers?' asked the ass.

'Who can be cheerful when he is out at elbows?' said the cat. 'I am getting on in years and my teeth are blunted, and I prefer to sit by the stove and purr instead of hunting round after mice. Just because of this my mistress wanted to drown me. I made myself scarce, but now I don't know where to turn.'

'Come with us to Bremen,' said the ass. 'You are a great hand at serenading, so you can become a town-musician.'

The cat consented, and joined them.

Next the fugitives passed by a yard where a cock was sitting on the door, crowing with all its might.

'You crow so loud you pierce one through and through,' said the ass. 'What is the matter?'

'Why! didn't I prophesy fine weather for Lady Day, when Our Lady washes the Christ Child's little garment and wants to dry it? But, notwithstanding this, because Sunday visitors are coming tomorrow, the mistress has no pity and she has ordered the cook to make me into soup, so I shall have my neck wrung tonight. Now I am crowing with all my might while I have the chance.'

'Come along, Red-comb,' said the ass; 'you had much better come with us. We are going to Bremen, and you will find a much better fate there. You have a good voice, and when we make music together there will be quality in it.'

The cock allowed himself to be persuaded, and they all four went off together. They could not, however, reach the town in one day, and by evening they arrived at a wood, where they determined to spend the night. The ass and the hound lay down under a big tree; the cat and the cock settled themselves in the branches, the cock flying right up to the top, which was the safest place for him. Before going to sleep he looked round once more in every direction; suddenly it seemed to him that he saw a light burning in the distance. He called out to his comrades that there must be a house not far off, for he saw a light:

'Very well,' said the ass, 'let us set out and make our way to it, for the entertainment here is very bad.'

The hound thought some bones or meat would suit him too, so they set out in the direction of the light, and soon saw it shining more clearly and getting bigger and bigger, till they reached a brightly-lighted robbers' den. The ass, being the tallest, approached the window and looked in.

'What do you see, old Jackass?' asked the cock.

'What do I see?' answered the ass, 'why, a table spread with delicious food and drink, and robbers seated at it enjoying themselves.'

'That would just suit us,' said the cock.

'Yes; if we were only there,' answered the ass.

Then the animals took counsel as to how to set about driving the robbers out. At last they hit upon a plan.

The ass was to take up his position with his forefeet on the window-sill, the hound was to jump on his back, the cat to climb up on to the hound, and last of all the cock flew up and perched on the cat's head. When they were thus arranged, at a given signal they all began to perform their music: the ass brayed, the hound barked, the cat mewed, and the cock crowed; then they dashed through the window, shivering the panes. The robbers jumped up at the terrible noise; they thought nothing less than that a demon was coming in upon them, and fled into the wood in the greatest alarm. Then the four animals sat down to table, and helped themselves according to taste, and ate as though they had been starving for weeks. When they had finished they extinguished the light and looked for sleeping places, each one to suit his nature and taste.

The ass lay down on the manure heap, the hound behind the door, the cat on the hearth near the warm ashes, and the cock flew up to the rafters. As they were tired from the long journey, they soon went to sleep.

When midnight was past, and the robbers saw from a distance that the light was no longer burning and that all seemed quiet, the chief said:

'We ought not to have been scared by a false alarm,' and ordered one of the robbers to go and examine the house.

Finding all quiet, the messenger went into the kitchen to kindle a light, and taking the cat's glowing, fiery eyes for live coals, he held a match close to them so as to light it. But the cat would stand no nonsense; it flew at his face, spat and scratched. He was terribly frightened and ran away.

He tried to get out by the back door, but the hound, who was lying there, jumped up and bit his leg. As he ran across the manure heap in front of the house, the ass gave him a good sound kick with his hind legs, while the cock, who had awoken at the uproar quite fresh and gay, cried out from his perch: 'Cock-a-doodle-doo.'

Thereupon the robber ran back as fast as he could to his chief, and said: 'There is a gruesome witch in the house, who breathed on me and scratched me with her long fingers. Behind the door there stands a man with a knife, who stabbed me; while in the yard lies a black monster, who hit me with a club; and upon the roof the judge is seated, and he called out, "Bring the rogue here," so I hurried away as fast as I could.'

Thenceforward the robbers did not venture again to the house, which, however, pleased the four Bremen musicians so much that they never wished to leave it again.

And he who last told the story has hardly finished speaking yet.

THE GOOSE-GIRL

There was once an old Queen whose husband had been dead for many years, and she had a very beautiful daughter. When she grew up she was betrothed to a Prince in a distant country. When the time came for the maiden to be sent into this distant country to be married, the old Queen packed up quantities of clothes and jewels, gold and silver, cups and ornaments, and, in fact, everything suitable to a royal outfit, for she loved her daughter very dearly.

She also sent a waiting-woman to travel with her, and to put her hand into that of the bridegroom. They each had a horse. The Princess's horse was called Falada, and it could speak.

When the hour of departure came, the old Queen went to her bedroom, and with a sharp little knife cut her finger and made it bleed. Then she held a piece of white cambric under it, and let three drops of blood fall on to it. This cambric she gave to her daughter, and said, 'Dear child, take good care of this; it will stand you in good stead on the journey.' They then bade each other a sorrowful farewell. The Princess hid the piece of cambric in her bosom, mounted her horse, and set out to her bridegroom's country.

When they had ridden for a time the Princess became very thirsty, and said to the waiting-woman, 'Get down and fetch me some water in my cup from the stream. I must have something to drink.'

'If you are thirsty,' said the waiting-woman, 'dismount yourself, lie down by the water and drink. I don't choose to be your servant.'

So, in her great thirst, the Princess dismounted and stooped down to the stream and drank, as she might not have her golden cup. The poor Princess said, 'Alas!' and the drops of blood answered, 'If your mother knew this, it would break her heart.'

The royal bride was humble, so she said nothing, but mounted her horse again. Then they rode several miles further; but the day was warm, the sun was scorching, and the Princess was soon thirsty again.

When they reached a river she called out once more to her waiting-woman, 'Get down, and give me some water in my golden cup!'

She had forgotten all about the rude words which had been said to her. But the waiting-woman answered more haughtily than ever, 'If you want to drink, get the water for yourself. I won't be your servant.'

Being very thirsty, the Princess dismounted, and knelt by the flowing water. She cried, and said, 'Ah me!' and the drops of blood answered, 'If your mother knew this, it would break her heart.'

While she stooped over the water to drink, the piece of cambric with the drops of blood on it fell out of her bosom and floated away on the stream; but she never noticed this in her great fear. The waiting-woman, however, had seen it, and rejoiced at getting more power over the bride, who, by losing the drops of blood, had become weak and powerless.

Now, when she was about to mount her horse Falada again, the waiting-woman said, 'By rights, Falada belongs to me; this jade will do for you!'

The poor Princess was obliged to give way. Then the waiting-woman, in a harsh voice, ordered her to take off her royal robes and to put on her own mean garments. Finally, she forced her to swear before heaven that she would not tell a creature at the Court what had taken place. Had she not taken the oath she would have been killed on the spot. But Falada saw all this and marked it.

The waiting-woman then mounted Falada and put the real bride on her poor jade, and they continued their journey.

There was great rejoicing when they arrived at the castle. The Prince hurried towards them, and lifted the waiting-woman from her horse, thinking she was his bride. She was led upstairs, but the real Princess had to stay below.

The old King looked out of the window and saw the delicate, pretty little creature standing in the courtyard; so he went to the bridal apartments and asked the bride about her companion who was left standing in the courtyard, and wished to know who she was.

'I picked her up on the way, and brought her with me for company. Give the girl something to do to keep her from idling.'

But the old King had no work for her, and could not think of anything. At last he said, 'I have a little lad who looks after the geese; she may help him.'

The boy was called little Conrad, and the real bride was sent with him to look after the geese.

Soon after, the false bride said to the Prince, 'Dear husband, I pray you do me a favour.' He answered, 'That will I gladly.'

'Well, then, let the knacker be called to cut off the head of the horse I rode; it angered me on the way.'

Really, she was afraid that the horse would speak, and tell of her treatment of the Princess. So it was settled, and the faithful Falada had to die.

When this came to the ear of the real Princess, she promised the knacker a piece of gold if he would do her a slight service. There was a great dark gateway to the town, through which she had to pass every morning and evening: would he nail up Falada's head in this gateway, so that she might see him as she passed?

The knacker promised to do as she wished, and when the horse's head was cut off, he hung it up in the dark gateway. In the early morning, when she and Conrad went through the gateway, she said in passing:

108

'Alas! dear Falada, there thou hangest!'

And the head answered:

'Alas! Queen's daughter, there thou gangest!
If thy mother knew thy fate,
Her heart would break with grief so great.'

Then they passed on out of the town, right into the fields, with the geese. When they reached the meadow, the Princess sat down on the grass and let down her hair. It shone like pure gold, and when little Conrad saw it, he was so delighted that he wanted to pluck some out; but she said:

'Blow, blow, little breeze,
And Conrad's hat seize.
Let him join in the chase
While away it is whirled,
Till my tresses are curled
And I rest in my place.'

Then a strong wind sprang up, which blew away Conrad's hat right over the fields, and he had to run after it. When he came back, she had finished combing her hair and it was all put up again; so he could not get a single hair. This made him very sulky, and he would not say another word to her. And they tended the geese till evening, when they went home.

Next morning, when they passed under the gateway, the Princess said:

'Alas! dear Falada, there thou hangest!'

Falada answered:

'Alas! Queen's daughter, there thou gangest!
If thy mother knew thy fate,
Her heart would break with grief so great.'

Again, when they reached the meadows, the Princess undid her hair and began combing it. Conrad ran to pluck some out but she said quickly:

'Blow, blow, little breeze,
And Conrad's hat seize.

Let him join in the chase
While away it is whirled,
Till my tresses are curled
And I rest in my place.'

The wind sprang up and blew Conrad's hat far away over the fields, and he had to run after it. When he came back the hair was all put up again, and he could not pull a single hair out. And they tended the geese till the evening. When they got home Conrad went to the old King, and said, 'I won't tend the geese with that maiden again.'

'Why not?' asked the King.

'Oh, she vexes me every day.'

The old King then ordered him to say what she did to vex him.

Conrad said, 'In the morning, when we pass under the dark gateway with the geese, she talks to a horse's head which is hung up on the wall. She says:

"Alas! Falada, there thou hangest!"

and the head answers:

"Alas! Queen's daughter, there thou gangest!
If thy mother knew thy fate,
Her heart would break with grief so great." '

Then Conrad went on to tell the King all that happened in the meadow, and how he had to run after his hat in the wind.

The old King ordered Conrad to go out next day as usual. Then he placed himself behind the dark gateway, and heard the Princess speaking to Falada's head. He also followed her into the field, and hid himself behind a bush, and with his own eyes he saw the goose-girl and the lad come driving the geese into the field. Then, after a time, he saw the girl let down her hair, which glittered in the sun. Directly after this, she said:

'Blow, blow, little breeze,
And Conrad's hat seize.
Let him join in the chase
While away it is whirled,
Till my tresses are curled
And I rest in my place.'

Then came a puff of wind, which carried off Conrad's hat and he had to run after it. While he was away, the maiden combed and did up her hair; and all this the old King observed. Thereupon he went away unnoticed; and in the evening, when the goose-girl came home, he called her aside and asked her why she did all these things.

'That I may not tell you, nor may I tell any human creature; for I have sworn it under the open sky, because if I had not done so I should have lost my life.'

He pressed her sorely, and gave her no peace, but he could get nothing out of her. Then he said, 'If you won't tell me, then tell your sorrows to the iron stove there,' and he went away.

She crept up to the stove, and, beginning to weep and lament, unburdened her heart to it, and said: 'Here I am, forsaken by all the world, and yet I am a Princess. A false waiting-woman brought me to such a pass that I had to take off my royal robes. Then she took my place with my bridegroom, while I have to do mean service as a goose-girl. If my mother knew this it would break her heart.'

The old King stood outside by the pipes of the stove, and heard all that she said. Then he came back and told her to go away from the stove. He caused royal robes to be put upon her, and her beauty was a marvel. The old King called his son, and told him that he had a false bride—she was only a waiting-woman; but the true bride was here, the so-called goose-girl.

The young Prince was charmed with her youth and beauty. A great banquet was prepared, to which all the courtiers and good friends were bidden. The bridegroom sat at the head of the table, with the Princess on one side and the waiting-woman at the other; but she was dazzled, and did not recognise the Princess in her brilliant apparel.

When they had eaten and drunk and were all very merry, the old King put a riddle to the waiting-woman. 'What does a person deserve who deceives his master?' telling the whole story, and ending by asking, 'What doom does he deserve?'

The false bride answered, 'No better than this. He must be put stark naked into a barrel stuck with nails, and be dragged along by two white horses from street to street till he is dead.'

'That is your own doom,' said the King, 'and the judgment shall be carried out.'

When the sentence was fulfilled, the young Prince married his true bride, and they ruled their kingdom together in peace and happiness.

There was once a father who had two sons. One was clever and sensible, and always knew how to get on. But the younger one was stupid, and could not learn anything, and he had no imagination.

When people saw him, they said: 'His father will have plenty of trouble with him.'

Whenever there was anything to be done, the eldest one always had to do it. But if his father sent him to fetch anything late in the evening, and the way lay through the churchyard or any other dreary place, he would answer: 'Oh no, father, not there; it makes me shudder!' For he was afraid.

In the evening, when stories were being told round the fire which made one's flesh creep, and the listeners said: 'Oh, you make me shudder!' the youngest son, sitting in the corner listening, could not imagine what they meant. 'They always say "It makes me shudder!" And it doesn't make me shudder a bit. It must be some art which I can't understand.'

Now it happened one day that his father said to him: 'I say, you in the corner there, you are growing big and strong. You must learn something by which you can earn a living. See what pains your brother takes, but you are not worth your salt.'

'Well, father,' he answered, 'I am quite ready to learn something; nay, I should very much like to learn how to shudder, for I know nothing about that.'

The elder son laughed when he heard him, and thought: 'Good heavens! what a fool my brother is; he will never do any good as long as he lives.'

But his father sighed, and answered: 'You will easily enough learn how to shudder, but you won't make your bread by it.'

Soon after, the sexton came to the house on a visit, and the father confided his troubles about his son to him. He told him how stupid he was, and how he could never learn anything. 'Would you believe that when I asked him how he was going to earn his living, he said he would like to learn how to shudder?'

'If that's all,' said the sexton, 'he may learn that from me. Just let me have him, and I'll soon put the polish on him.'

The father was pleased, for he thought: 'Anyhow, the lad will gain something by it.'

So the sexton took him home with him, and he had to ring the church-bells.

A few days after, the sexton woke him at midnight and told him to get up and ring the bells. 'You shall soon be taught how to shudder!' he thought, as he crept stealthily up the stairs beforehand.

When the lad got up into the tower and turned round to catch hold of the bell rope, he saw a white figure standing on the steps opposite the belfry window.

'Who is there?' he cried; but the figure neither moved nor answered.

'Answer,' cried the lad, 'or get out of the way. You have no business here in the night.'

But so that the lad should think he was a ghost, the sexton did not stir.

The lad cried for the second time: 'What do you want here? Speak if you are an honest fellow, or I'll throw you down the stairs.'

The sexton did not think he would go to such lengths, so he made no sound, and stood as still as if he were made of stone.

Then the lad called to him the third time, and, as he had no answer, he took a run and threw the ghost down the stairs. It fell down ten steps and remained lying in a corner.

Then he rang the bells, went home, and, without saying a word to anybody, went to bed and was soon fast asleep.

The sexton's wife waited a long time for her husband, but, as he never came back, she got frightened, and woke up the lad.

'Don't you know what has become of my husband?' she asked. 'He went up into the church tower before you.'

'No,' answered the lad. 'There was somebody standing on the stairs opposite the belfry window, and, as he would neither answer me nor go away, I took him to be a rogue and threw him downstairs. Go and see if it was your husband; I should be sorry if it were.'

The woman hurried away and found her husband lying in the corner, moaning with a broken leg. She carried him down, and then hastened with loud cries to the lad's father.

'Your son has brought about a great misfortune; he has thrown my husband downstairs and broken his leg. Take the good-for-nothing fellow away, out of our house.'

The father was horrified, and, going back with her, gave the lad a good scolding.

'What is the meaning of this inhuman prank? The Evil One must have put it into your head.'

'Father,' answered the lad, 'just listen to me. I am quite innocent. He stood there in the dark, like a man with some wicked design. I did not know who it was, and I warned him three times to speak, or to go away!'

'Alas!' said his father, 'you bring me nothing but disaster. Go away out of my sight. I will have nothing more to do with you.'

'Gladly, father. Only wait till daylight; then I will go away, and learn to shudder. Then, at least, I shall have one art to make my living by.'

'Learn what you like,' said his father. 'It's all the same to me. Here are fifty thalers for you. Go out into the world, and don't tell a creature where you come from, or who your father is, for you will only bring me to shame.'

'Just as you please, father. If that is all you want, I can easily fulfil your desire.'

At daybreak, the lad put his fifty thalers into his pocket and went out along the high road, repeating over and over to himself as he went: 'If only I could shudder, if only I could shudder.'

A man came by and overheard the words the lad was saying to himself, and when they had gone a little further, and came within sight of the gallows, he said; 'See, there is the tree where those seven have been wedded to the ropemaker's daughter, and are now learning to fly. Sit down below them, and when night comes you will soon learn to shudder.'

'If nothing more than that is needed,' said the lad, 'it is easily done. And if I learn to shudder as easily as that, you shall have my fifty thalers. Come back to me early tomorrow morning.'

Then the lad went up to the gallows, and sat down under them to wait till night came.

As he was cold he lighted a fire, but at midnight the wind grew so cold that he did not know how to keep himself warm. The wind blew the men on the gallows backwards and forwards, and swung them against each other, so he thought: 'Here am I freezing by the fire, how much colder they must be up there.'

And as he was very compassionate, he mounted the ladder, undid them, and brought all seven down, one by one. Then he blew up the fire, and placed them round it to warm themselves. They sat there and never moved, even when the fire caught their clothing.

'Take care, or I will hang you all up again.'

The dead men, of course, could not hear, and remained silent while their few rags were burnt up.

Then he grew angry, and said: 'If you won't take care of yourselves, I can't help you, and I won't be burnt with you.'

So he hung them all up again in a row, and sat down by the fire and went to sleep again. Next morning, the man, wanting to get his fifty thalers, came to him and said: 'Now do you know what shuddering means?'

'No,' he said, 'how should I have learnt it? Those fellows up there never opened their mouths, and they were so stupid they let the few poor rags they had about them burn.'

Then the man saw that no thalers would be his that day, and he went away, saying: 'Never in my life have I seen such a fellow as this.'

The lad also went on his way, and again began saying to himself: 'Oh, if only I could learn to shudder, if only I could learn to shudder.'

A carter, walking behind him, heard this, and asked: 'Who are you?'

'I don't know,' answered the youth.

'Who is your father?'

'That I must not say.'

'What are you always mumbling in your beard?'

'Ah,' answered the youth, 'I want to learn to shudder, but no one can teach me.'

'Stop your silly chatter,' said the carter. 'Just you come with me, and I'll see that you have what you want.'

The youth went with the carter, and in the evening they reached an inn, where they meant to pass the night. He said, quite loud, as they entered: 'Oh, if only I could learn to shudder, if only I could learn to shudder.'

The landlord, who heard him, laughed, and said: 'If that's what you want, there should be plenty of opportunity for you here.'

'I will have nothing to say to it,' said the landlady. 'So many a prying fellow has already paid the penalty with his life. It would be a sin and a shame if those bright eyes should not see the light of day again.'

But the youth said: 'I will learn it somehow, however hard it may be. I have been driven out for not knowing it.'

He gave the landlord no peace till he told him that there was an enchanted castle a little way off, where anyone could be made to shudder if he would pass three nights in it. The King had promised his daughter to wife to anyone who dared do it, and she was the prettiest maiden the sun had ever shone on. There were also great treasures hidden in the castle, watched over by evil spirits, enough to make any poor man rich who could break the spell. Already many had gone in, but none had ever come out.

Next morning the youth went to the King, and said: 'By your leave, I should like to spend three nights in the enchanted castle.'

The King looked at him, and, as he took a fancy to him, he said: 'You may ask three things to take into the castle with you, but they must be lifeless things.'

He answered: 'Then I ask for a fire, a turning-lathe, and a cooper's bench with the knife.'

The King had all three carried into the castle with him.

When night fell, the youth went up to the castle and made a bright fire in one of the rooms. He put the cooper's bench with the knife near to the fire, and seated himself on the turning-lathe.

'Oh, if only I could shudder,' he said, 'but I shan't learn it here either.'

Towards midnight he wanted to make up the fire, and as he was blowing it up, something in one corner began to shriek: 'Miau, miau, how cold we are!'

'You fools!' he cried. 'What do you shriek for? If you are cold, come and warm yourselves by the fire.'

As he spoke, two big black cats bounded up and sat down, one on each side of him, and stared at him with wild, fiery eyes.

After a time, when they had warmed themselves, they said: 'Comrade, shall we have a game of cards?'

'Why not?' he answered, 'but show me your paws first.'

Then they stretched out their claws.

'Why,' he said, 'what long nails you've got. Wait a bit; I must cut them for you.'

He seized them by the scruff of their necks, lifted them on to the cooper's bench, and screwed their paws firmly to it.

'I have looked at your fingers, and the desire to play cards with you has passed.'

Then he killed them and threw them out into the moat.

But no sooner had he got rid of these two cats, and was about to sit down by his fire again, than crowds of black cats and dogs swarmed out of every corner, more and more of them. They howled horribly, and trampled on his fire, and tried to put it out.

For a time he looked quietly on, but when it grew too bad he scized his cooper's knife and cried: 'Away with you, you rascally pack,' and let fly among them right and left. Some of them sprang away; the others he killed and threw out into the water.

When he came back he scraped the embers of his fire together again, and warmed himself. He could hardly keep his eyes open, and felt the greatest desire to go to sleep. He looked round, and in one corner he saw a big bed.

'That's the very thing,' he said, and lay down in it. As soon as he closed his eyes the bed began to move, and soon it was tearing round and round the castle. 'Very good!' he said. 'The faster the better!' The bed rolled on as if it were dragged by six horses—over thresholds and stairs, up and down.

Suddenly it went hop, hop, hop, and turned topsy-turvy, so that it lay upon him like a mountain. But he pitched the pillows and blankets into the air, slipped out of it, and said: 'Now anyone may ride who likes.'

Then he lay down by his fire and slept till daylight.

In the morning the King came, and when he saw him lying on the floor, he thought the ghosts had killed him and he was dead. So he said: 'It's a sad pity for such a handsome fellow.'

But the youth heard him and sat up, saying: 'It has not come to that yet.'

The King was surprised and delighted, and asked him how he had got on.

'Pretty well!' he answered. 'One night is gone; I suppose I shall get through the others too.'

When the landlord saw him he opened his eyes and said: 'I never thought I should see you alive again. Have you learnt how to shudder now?'

'No,' he answered, 'it's all in vain. If only someone would tell me how.'

The second night came, and up he went again and sat down by the fire and began his old song: 'Oh, if only I could learn to shudder.'

In the middle of the night a great noise and uproar began, first soft, and then growing louder; then for a short time there would be silence.

At last, with a loud scream, half the body of a man fell down the chimney in front of him.

'Hullo!' he said, 'another half is wanting here; this is too little.'

The noise began again, and, amidst shrieks and howls, the other half fell down.

'Wait a bit,' he said, 'I'll blow up the fire.'

When this was done, and he looked round, the two halves had come together, and a hideous man sat in his place.

'We didn't bargain for that,' said the youth. 'The bench is mine.'

The man wanted to push him out of the way, but the youth would not have it, flung him aside, and took his own seat.

Then more men fell down the chimney, one after the other, and they fetched nine human shin-bones and two skulls, and began to play skittles. The youth felt inclined to join them, and cried: 'I say, can I play too?'

'Yes, if you've got any money.'

'Money enough,' he answered, 'but your balls aren't quite round.'

Then he took the skulls and turned them on the lathe till they were· quite round. 'Now they will roll better,' he said. 'Here goes! The more, the merrier!'

So he played with them and lost some money, but when it struck twelve everything disappeared. He lay down and was soon fast asleep.

Next morning the King came again to look after him, and said: 'Well, how did you get on this time?'

'I played skittles,' he answered, 'and lost a few coins.'

'Didn't you learn to shudder?'

'Not I. I only made merry. Oh, if I could but find out how to shudder.'

On the third night he again sat down on his bench, and said quite savagely: 'If only I could shudder!'

When it grew late, six tall men came in carrying a bier, and he said: 'Hullo there! That must be my cousin who died a few days ago.' And he beckoned and said: 'Come along, cousin, come along.'

The men put the coffin on the floor, and he went up and took the lid off, and there lay a dead man. He felt the face, and it was as cold as ice. 'Wait,' he said, 'I will warm him.'

Then he went to the fire and warmed his hand and laid it on the dead man's face, but the dead man remained cold. He took him out of the coffin, sat down by the fire and took him on his knees, and rubbed his arms to make the blood circulate.

But it was all no good. Next, it came into his head that if two people were in bed together, they warmed each other. So he put the dead man in the bed, covered him up, and lay down beside him.

After a time the dead man grew warm and began to move.

Then the youth said: 'There, you see, cousin mine, have I not warmed you?'

But the man rose up and cried: 'Now I will strangle you!'

'What!' said he, 'are those all the thanks I get? Back you go into your coffin then.' So saying, he lifted him up, threw him in, and fastened down the lid. Then the six men came back and carried the coffin away.

'I cannot shudder,' he said, 'and I shall never learn it here.'

Just then a huge man appeared. He was frightful to look at, old, and with a long white beard.

'Oh, you miserable wight!' he cried. 'You shall soon learn what shuddering is, for you shall die.'

'Not so fast,' said the youth. 'If I am to die, I must be present.'

'I will make short work of you,' said the old monster.

'Softly! softly! don't you boast. I am as strong as you, and very likely much stronger.'

'We shall see about that,' said the old man. 'If you are the stronger, I will let you go. Come; we will try.'

Then he led him through numberless dark passages to a smithy, took an axe, and with one blow struck one of the anvils into the earth.

'I can better that,' said the youth, and went to the other anvil. The old man placed himself near to see, and his white beard hung over.

Then the youth took the axe and split the anvil with one blow, catching the old man's beard in it at the same time.

'Now, I have you fast,' said the youth, 'and you will be the one to die.'

Then he seized an iron rod and belaboured the old man with it till he shrieked for mercy, and promised him great riches if he would stop.

Then the youth pulled out the axe and released him, and the old man led him back into the castle and showed him three chests of gold in a cellar.

'One is for the poor,' he said, 'one for the King, and one for you.'

The clock struck twelve, and the ghost disappeared, leaving the youth in the dark.

'I must manage to get out somehow,' he said, and groped about till he found his way back to his room, where he lay down by the fire and went to sleep.

Next morning the King came and said: 'Now you must have learnt how to shudder.'

'No,' said he. 'What can it be? My dead cousin was there, and an old man with a beard came and showed me a lot of gold. But what shuddering is, that no man can tell me.'

Then said the King: 'You have broken the spell on the castle, and you shall marry my daughter.'

'That is all very well,' he said; 'but still I don't know what shuddering is.'

The gold was got out of the castle, and the marriage was celebrated, but, happy as the young King was, and much as he loved his wife, he was always saying: 'Oh, if only I could learn to shudder, if only I could learn to shudder.'

At last his wife was vexed by it, and her waiting-woman said: 'I can help you; he shall be taught the meaning of shuddering.'

And she went out to the brook that ran through the garden and got a pail full of cold water and little fishes.

At night, when the young King was asleep, his wife took the coverings off and poured the cold water over him, and all the little fishes flopped about him.

Then he woke up, and cried: 'Oh, how I am shuddering, dear wife, how I am shuddering! Now I know what shuddering is!'

Once there was a miller who was poor, but who had a beautiful daughter. Now it happened that he had to go and speak to the King, and in order to make himself appear important he said to him, 'I have a daughter who can spin straw into gold.'

The King said to the miller, 'That is an art which pleases me well; if your daughter is as clever as you say, bring her tomorrow to my palace, and I will try what she can do.'

And when the girl was brought to him he took her into a room which was quite full of straw, gave her a spinning-wheel and a reel, and said, 'Now set to work, and if by tomorrow morning early you have not spun this straw into gold during the night, you must die.' Thereupon he himself locked up the room, and left her in it alone. So there sat the poor miller's daughter, and for her life could not tell what to do; she had no idea how straw could be spun into gold, and she grew more and more miserable, until at last she began to weep.

But all at once the door opened, and in came a little man and said, 'Good evening, Mistress Miller; why are you crying so?'

'Alas!' answered the girl, 'I have to spin straw into gold, and I do not know how to do it.'

'What will you give me,' said the manikin, 'if I do it for you?'

'My necklace,' said the girl.

The little man took the necklace, seated himself in front of the wheel, and whirr, whirr, whirr, three turns, and the reel was full; then he put another on, and whirr, whirr, whirr, three times round, and the second was full too. And so it went on until the morning, when all the straw was spun and all the reels were full of gold.

By daybreak the King was already there, and when he saw the gold he was astonished and delighted, but his heart became only more greedy. He had the miller's daughter taken into another room full of straw, which was much larger, and commanded her to spin that also in one night if she valued her life. The girl knew not how to help herself, and was crying, when the door again opened, and the little man appeared, and said, 'What will you give me if I spin the straw into gold for you?'

'The ring on my finger,' answered the girl.

The little man took the ring, again began to turn the wheel, and by morning had spun all the straw into glittering gold.

The King rejoiced beyond measure at the sight, but still he had not gold enough; and he had the miller's daughter taken into a still larger room full of straw, and said, 'You must spin this, too, in the course of this night; but if you succeed, you shall be my wife.'

'Even if she be a miller's daughter,' thought he, 'I could not find a richer wife in the whole world.'

When the girl was alone the manikin came again for the third time, and said, 'What will you give me if I spin the straw for you this time also?'

'I have nothing left that I could give,' answered the girl.

'Then promise me, if you should become Queen, your first child.'

'Who knows whether that will ever happen?' thought the miller's daughter; and, not knowing how else to help herself in this strait, she promised the manikin what he wanted, and for that he once more spun the straw into gold.

And when the King came in the morning and found all as he had wished, he took her in marriage, and the pretty miller's daughter became a Queen.

A year after, she had a beautiful child, and she never gave a thought to the manikin. But suddenly he came into her room, and said, 'Now give me what you promised.'

The Queen was horror-struck, and offered the manikin all the riches of the kingdom if he would leave her the child.

But the manikin said, 'No, something that is living is dearer to me than all the treasures of the world.'

Then the Queen began to weep and cry, so that the manikin pitied her. 'I will give you three days' time,' said he; 'if by that time you find out my name, then you shall keep your child.'

So the Queen thought the whole night of all the names that she had ever heard, and she sent a messenger to inquire, far and wide, for any other names that there might be. When the manikin came the next day, she began with Caspar, Melchior, Balthazar, and said all the names she knew, one after another; but to every one the little man said, 'That is not my name.'

On the second day she had enquiries made in the neighbourhood as to the names of all the people there, and she repeated to the manikin the most uncommon and curious. 'Perhaps your name is Shortribs, or Sheepshanks, or Laceleg?' but he always answered, 'That is not my name.'

On the third day the messenger came back again, and said, 'I have not been able to find a single new name, but as I came to a high mountain at the end of the forest, where the fox and the hare bid each other good night, there I saw a little house, and before the house a fire was burning, and round about the fire quite a ridiculous little man was jumping; he hopped upon one leg, and shouted:

' "Today I bake, tomorrow I brew,
    The next I'll have the young Queen's child.

Ha! glad am I that no one knew,
That Rumpelstiltskin I am styled." '

You may think how glad the Queen was when she heard the name! And when soon afterwards the little man came in and asked, 'Now, Mistress Queen, what is my name?' at first she said, 'Is your name Conrad?'

'No.'

'Is your name Harry?'

'No.'

'Perhaps your name is Rumpelstiltskin?'

'The Devil has told you that! the Devil has told you that!' cried the little man, and in his anger he plunged his right foot so deep into the earth that his whole leg went in; and then in rage he pulled at his left leg so hard with both hands that he tore himself in two.

BEARSKIN

There was once a young fellow who enlisted as a soldier, conducted himself bravely, and was always the foremost when it rained bullets. So long as the war lasted, all went well, but when peace was made he received his dismissal, and the captain said he might go where he liked. His parents were dead, and he had no longer a home, so he went to his brothers and begged them to take him in, and keep him until war broke out again. The brothers, however, were hard-hearted, and said, 'What can we do with you? You are of no use to us; go and make a living for yourself.'

The soldier had nothing left but his gun; he took that on his shoulder, and went forth into the world. He came to a wide heath on which nothing was to be seen but a circle of trees; under these he sat sorrowfully down, and began to think over his fate. 'I have no money,' thought he, 'I have learnt no trade but that of fighting, and now that they have made peace they don't want me any longer; so I see beforehand that I shall have to starve.'

All at once he heard a rustling, and when he looked round, a strange man stood before him, who wore a green coat and looked right stately, but had a hideous cloven foot. 'I know already what thou art in need of,' said the man, 'gold and possessions shalt thou have, as much as thou canst make away with, do what thou wilt, but first I must know if thou art fearless, that I may not bestow my money in vain.'

'A soldier and fear—how can those two things go together?' he answered; 'thou canst put me to the proof.'

'Very well, then,' answered the man, 'look behind thee.'

The soldier turned round and saw a large bear, which came growling towards him. 'Oho!' cried the soldier, 'I will tickle your nose for you, so that you shall soon lose your fancy for growling,' and he aimed at the bear and shot it through the muzzle; if fell down and never stirred again.

'I see quite well,' said the stranger, 'that thou art not wanting in courage, but there is still another condition which thou wilt have to fulfil.'

'If it does not endanger my salvation,' replied the soldier, who knew very well who was standing by him. 'If it does, I will have nothing to do with it.'

'Thou wilt look to that for thyself,' answered Greencoat; 'thou shalt for the next seven years neither wash thyself, nor comb thy beard, nor thy hair, nor cut thy nails, nor say one paternoster. I will give thee a coat and a cloak, which during this time thou must wear. If thou diest during these seven years, thou art mine; if thou remainest alive, thou art free, and rich to boot, for all the rest of thy life.'

The soldier thought of the great extremity in which he now found himself, and as he had so often gone to meet death, he resolved to risk it now also, and agreed to the terms.

The Devil took off his green coat, gave it to the soldier, and said, 'If thou hast this coat on thy back and puttest thy hand into the pocket, thou wilt always find it full of money.' Then he pulled the skin off the bear, and said, 'This shall be thy cloak, and thy bed also, for thereon thou shalt sleep, and in no other bed shalt thou lie, and because of this apparel shalt thou be called Bearskin.' After this the Devil vanished.

The soldier put the coat on, felt at once in the pocket, and found that the thing was really true. Then he put on the bearskin and went forth into the world, and enjoyed himself, refraining from nothing that did him good and his money harm.

During the first year, his appearance was passable, but during the second he began to look like a monster. His hair covered nearly the whole of his face, his beard was like a piece of coarse felt, his fingers had claws, and his face was so covered with dirt that if cress had been sown on it, it would have come up. Whosoever saw him, ran away, but as he everywhere gave the poor money to pray that he might not die during the seven years, and as he paid well for everything, he still always found shelter.

In the fourth year, he entered an inn where the landlord would not receive him, and would not even let him have a place in the stable because he was afraid the horses would be scared. But as Bearskin thrust his hand into his pocket and pulled out a handful of ducats, the host let himself be persuaded and gave him a room in an outhouse. Bearskin was, however, obliged to promise not to let himself be seen, lest the inn should get a bad name.

As Bearskin was sitting alone in the evening, and wishing from the bottom of his heart that the seven years were over, he heard a loud lamenting in a neighbouring room. He had a compassionate heart, so he opened the door, and saw an old man weeping bitterly and wringing his hands. Bearskin went nearer, but the man sprang to his feet and tried to escape from him. At last, when the man perceived that Bearskin's voice was human, he let himself be prevailed on, and by kind words Bearskin succeeded so far that the old man revealed the cause of his grief. His property had dwindled away by degrees, he and his daughters would have to starve, and he was so poor that he could not pay the innkeeper and was to be put in prison.

'If that is your only trouble,' said Bearskin, 'I have plenty of money.' He caused the innkeeper to be brought thither, paid him, and put a purse full of gold into the poor old man's pocket besides.

When the old man saw himself set free from all his troubles he did not know how to be grateful enough. 'Come with me,' said he to Bearskin. 'My daughters are all miracles of beauty; choose one of them for yourself as a wife. When she hears what you have done for me, she will not refuse you. You do in truth look a little strange, but she will soon put you to rights again.'

This pleased Bearskin well, and he went.

When the eldest saw him she was so terribly alarmed at his face that she screamed and ran away.

The second stood still and looked at him from head to foot, but then she said, 'How can I accept a husband who no longer has a human form? The shaven bear that once was here and passed itself off for a man pleased me far better, for at any rate it wore a hussar's dress and white gloves. If it were nothing but ugliness, I might get used to that.'

The youngest, however, said, 'Dear father, that must be a good man to have helped you out of your trouble, so if you have promised him a bride for doing it, your promise must be kept.'

It was a pity that Bearskin's face was covered with dirt and with hair, for, if not, they might have seen how delighted he was when he heard these words. He took a ring from his finger, broke it in two, and gave her one half; the other he kept for himself. He wrote his name, however, on her half, and hers on his, and begged her to keep her piece carefully, and then he took his leave and said, 'I must still wander about for three years, and if I do not return then, you are free, for I shall be dead. But pray to God to preserve my life.'

The poor betrothed bride dressed herself entirely in black, and when she thought of her future bridegroom, tears came into her eyes. Nothing but contempt and mockery fell to her lot from her sisters. 'Take care,' said the eldest, 'if you give him your hand, he will strike his claws into it.'

'Beware!' said the second. 'Bears like sweet things, and if he takes a fancy to you, he will eat you up.'

'You must always do as he likes,' began the elder again, 'or else he will growl.'

And the second continued, 'But the wedding will be a merry one, for bears dance well.'

The bride was silent and did not let them vex her. Bearskin, however, travelled about the world from one place to another, did good where he was able, and gave generously to the poor, that they might pray for him.

At length, as the last day of the seven years dawned, he went once more out on to the heath, and seated himself beneath the circle of trees. It was not long before the wind whistled, and the Devil stood before him and looked angrily at him; then he threw Bearskin his old coat, and asked for his own green one back. 'We have not got so far as that yet,' answered Bearskin, 'thou must first make me clean.' Whether the Devil liked it or not, he was forced to fetch water and wash

Bearskin, comb his hair, and cut his nails. After this, he looked like a brave soldier, and was much handsomer than he had ever been before.

When the Devil had gone away, Bearskin was quite light-hearted. He went into the town, put on a magnificent velvet coat, seated himself in a carriage drawn by four white horses, and drove to his bride's house. No one recognised him; the father took him for a distinguished general, and led him into the room where his daughters were sitting. He was forced to place himself between the two eldest; they helped him to wine, gave him the best pieces of meat, and thought that in all the world they had never seen a handsomer man. The bride, however, sat opposite to him in her black dress and never raised her eyes, nor spoke a word. When at length he asked the father if he would give him one of his daughters to wife, the two eldest jumped up and ran into their bedrooms to put on splendid dresses, for each of them fancied she was the chosen one.

The stranger, as soon as he was alone with his bride, brought out his half of the ring and threw it in a glass of wine which he reached across the table to her. She took the wine, but when she had drunk it and found the ring lying at the bottom, her heart began to beat. She got the other half, which she wore on a ribbon round her neck, joined them, and saw that the two pieces fitted exactly together. Then said he, 'I am your betrothed bridegroom, whom you saw as Bearskin, but through God's grace I have again received my human form, and have once more become clean.' He went up to her, embraced her, and gave her a kiss.

In the meantime, the two sisters came back in full dress, and when they saw that the handsome man had fallen to the share of the youngest, and heard that he was Bearskin, they ran out full of anger and rage. One of them drowned herself in the well, the other hanged herself on a tree.

In the evening, someone knocked at the door, and when the bridegroom opened it, it was the Devil in his green coat, who said, 'Seest thou, I have now got two souls in the place of thy one!'

JORINDA AND JORINGEL

There was once an old castle in the middle of a vast thick wood; in it there lived an old woman quite alone, and she was a witch. By day she made herself into a cat or a screech-owl, but regularly at night she became a human being again. In this way she was able to decoy wild beasts and birds, which she would kill, and boil or roast. If any man came within a hundred paces of the castle, he was forced to stand still and could not move from the place till she gave the word of release; but if an innocent maiden came within the circle, she changed her into a bird, and shut her up in a cage which she carried into a room in the castle. She must have had seven thousand cages of this kind, containing pretty birds.

Now, there was once a maiden called Jorinda who was more beautiful than all other maidens. She had promised to marry a very handsome youth named Joringel, and it was in the days of their courtship, when they took the greatest joy in being alone together, that one day they wandered out into the forest. 'Take care,' said Joringel; 'do not let us go too near the castle.'

It was a lovely evening. The sunshine glanced between the tree-trunks of the dark greenwood, while the turtle-doves sang plaintively in the old beech trees. Yet Jorinda sat down in the sunshine and could not help weeping and bewailing, while Joringel, too, soon became just as mournful. They both felt miserable as if they had been going to die. Gazing round them, they found they had lost their way, and did not know how they should find the path home.

Half the sun still appeared above the mountain; half had sunk below. Joringel peered into the bushes and saw the old walls of the castle quite close to them; he was terror-struck, and became pale as death. Jorinda was singing:

'My birdie with its ring so red
Sings sorrow, sorrow, sorrow;
My love will mourn when I am dead,
Tomorrow, morrow, mor—jug, jug.'

Joringel looked at her, but she was changed into a nightingale who sang 'Jug, jug.'

A screech-owl with glowing eyes flew three times round her, and cried three times 'Shu hu-hu.' Joringel could not stir; he stood like a stone without being able to speak, or cry, or move hand or foot. The sun had now set. The owl flew into a bush, out of which appeared almost at the same moment a crooked old woman, skinny and yellow; she had big, red eyes and a crooked nose whose tip reached her chin. She mumbled something, caught the nightingale, and carried it away in her hand. Joringel could not say a word nor move from the spot, and the nightingale was gone. At last the old woman came back, and said in a droning voice: 'Greeting to thee, Zachiel! When the moon shines upon the cage, unloose the captive, Zachiel!'

Then Joringel was free. He fell on his knees before the witch, and implored her to give back his Jorinda; but she said he should never have her again, and went away. He pleaded, he wept, he lamented, but all in vain. 'Alas! what is to become of me?' said Joringel.

Finally he went away, and arrived at a strange village, where he spent a long time as a shepherd. He often wandered round about the castle, but did not go too near it. At last he dreamt one night that he found a blood-red flower, in the midst of which was a beautiful large pearl. He plucked the flower, and took it to the castle. Whatever he touched with it was made free of enchantment. He dreamt, too, that by this means he had found his Jorinda again.

In the morning when he awoke he began to search over hill and dale, in the hope of finding a flower like this; he searched till the ninth day, when he found the flower early in the morning. In the middle was a big dewdrop, as big as the finest pearl. This flower he carried day and night, till he reached the castle. He was not held fast as before when he came within the hundred paces of the castle, but walked straight up to the door.

Joringel was filled with joy; he touched the door with the flower, and it flew open. He went in through the court, and listened for the sound of birds. He went on and found the hall, where the witch was feeding the birds in the seven thousand cages. When she saw Joringel she was angry, very angry—scolded, and spat poison and gall at him. He paid no attention to her, but turned away and searched among the bird-cages. Yes, but there were many hundred nightingales; how was he to find his Jorinda?

While he was looking about in this way he noticed that the old woman was secretly removing a cage with a bird inside, and was making for the door. He sprang swiftly towards her, touched the cage and the witch with the flower, and then she no longer had power to exercise her spells. Jorinda stood there, as beautiful as before, and threw her arms round Joringel's neck. After that he changed all the other birds back into maidens again, and went home with Jorinda, and they lived long and happily together.

MOTHER HOLLE

There was once a widow who had two daughters—one of whom was pretty and industrious, whilst the other was ugly and idle. But she was much fonder of the ugly and idle one, because she was her own daughter; and the other, who was a stepdaughter, was obliged to do all the work, and be the Cinderella of the house. Every day the poor girl had to sit by a well in the highway, and spin and spin till her fingers bled.

Now it happened that one day the shuttle was marked with her blood, so she dipped it in the well, to wash the mark off; but it dropped out of her hand and fell to the bottom. She began to weep, and ran to her stepmother and told her of the mishap. But she scolded her sharply, and was so merciless as to say, 'Since you have let the shuttle fall in, you must fetch it out again.'

So the girl went back to the well and did not know what to do; and in the sorrow of her heart she jumped into the well to get the shuttle. She lost her senses; and when she awoke and came to herself again, she was in a lovely meadow where the sun was shining and many thousands of flowers were growing. Along this meadow she went, and at last came to a baker's oven full of bread, and the bread cried out, 'Oh, take me out! take me out! or I shall burn; I have been baked a long time!' So she went up to it, and took out all the loaves one after the other with the bread shovel.

After that she went on till she came to a tree covered with apples, which called out to her, 'Oh, shake me! shake me! we apples are all ripe!' So she shook the tree till the apples fell like rain, and went on shaking till they were all down, and when she had gathered them into a heap, she went on her way.

At last she came to a little house, out of which an old woman peeped; but she had such large teeth that the girl was frightened, and was about to run away. But the old woman called out to her, 'What are you afraid of, dear child? Stay with me; if you will do all the work in the house properly, you shall be the better for it. Only you must take care to make my bed well, and to shake it thoroughly till the feathers fly—for then there is snow on the earth. I am Mother Holle.'

As the old woman spoke so kindly to her, the girl took courage and agreed to enter her service. She attended to everything to the satisfaction of her mistress, and always shook her bed so vigorously that the feathers flew about like snow-flakes. So she had a pleasant life with her; never an angry word and boiled or roast meat every day.

She stayed some time with Mother Holle, and then she became sad. At first she did not know what was the matter with her, but found at length that it was homesickness; although she was many thousand times better off here than at home, still she had a longing to be there. At last she said to the old woman, 'I have a longing for home, and however well off I am down here, I cannot stay any longer; I must go up again to my own people.'

Mother Holle said, 'I am pleased that you long for your home, and as you have served me so truly, I myself will take you up again.' Thereupon she took her by the hand, and led her to a large door. The door was opened, and just as the maiden was standing beneath the doorway, a heavy shower of golden rain fell, and all the gold remained sticking to her, so that she was completely covered over with it.

'You shall have that because you are so industrious,' said Mother Holle; and at the same time she gave her back the shuttle which she had let fall into the well. Thereupon the door closed, and the maiden found herself up above upon the earth, not far from her mother's house.

And as she went into the yard the cock was standing by the well-side, and cried:

'Cock-a-doodle-doo!
Your golden girl's come back to you!'

So she went in to her mother, and as she arrived thus covered with gold, she was well received, both by her and her sister.

The girl told all that had happened to her; and as soon as the mother heard how she had come by so much wealth, she was very anxious to obtain the same good luck for the ugly and lazy daughter, who now had to seat herself by the well and spin. And in order that the shuttle might be stained with blood, she stuck her hand into a thorn bush and pricked her finger. Then she threw her shuttle into the well, and jumped in after it.

She came, like the other, to the beautiful meadow and walked along the very same path. When she got to the oven the bread again cried, 'Oh, take me out! take me out! or I shall burn; I have been baked a long time!' But the lazy thing answered, 'As if I had any wish to make myself dirty?' and on she went.

Soon she came to the apple tree, which cried, 'Oh, shake me! shake me! we apples are all ripe!' But she answered, 'I like that! one of you might fall on my head,' and so went on.

When she came to Mother Holle's house she was not afraid, for she had already heard of her big teeth, and she hired herself to her immediately.

The first day she forced herself to work diligently, and obeyed Mother Holle when she told her to do anything, for she was thinking of all the gold that she would give her. But on the second day she began to be lazy, and on the third day still more so, and then she would not get up in the morning at all. Neither did

she make Mother Holle's bed as she ought, and did not shake it so as to make the feathers fly up.

Mother Holle was soon tired of this, and gave her notice to leave. The lazy girl was willing enough to go, and thought that now the golden rain would come. Mother Holle led her, too, to the great door; but while she was standing beneath it, instead of the gold a big kettleful of pitch was emptied over her. 'That is the reward of your service,' said Mother Holle, and shut the door.

So the lazy girl went home; but she was quite covered with pitch, and the cock by the well-side, as soon as he saw her, cried out:

'Cock-a-doodle-doo!
Your pitchy girl's come back to you!'

But the pitch stuck fast to her, and could not be got off as long as she lived.

There was once a poor widow who lived in a lonely cottage. In front of the cottage was a garden wherein stood two rose-trees, one of which bore white and the other red roses. She had two children who were like the two rose-trees, and one was called Snow-white and the other Rose-red. They were as good and happy, as busy and cheerful as ever two children in the world were, only Snow-white was more quiet and gentle than Rose-red. Rose-red liked better to run about in the meadows and fields seeking flowers and catching butterflies; but Snow-white sat at home with her mother, and helped her with her housework, or read to her when there was nothing to do.

The two children were so fond of each other that they always held each other by the hand when they went out together, and when Snow-white said, 'We will not leave each other,' Rose-red answered, 'Never so long as we live,' and their mother would add, 'What one has she must share with the other.'

They often ran about the forest alone and gathered red berries, and no beasts did them any harm, but came close to them trustfully. The little hare would eat a cabbage-leaf out of their hands, the roe grazed by their side, the stag leapt merrily by them, and the birds sat still upon the boughs and sang whatever they knew.

No mishap overtook them; if they stayed too late in the forest, and night came on, they laid themselves down near one another upon the moss and slept until morning came, and their mother knew this and had no distress on their account.

Once when they had spent the night in the wood and the dawn had roused them, they saw a beautiful child in a shining white dress sitting near their bed. He got up and looked quite kindly at them, but said nothing and went away into the forest. And when they looked round they found that they had been sleeping quite close to a precipice, and would certainly have fallen into it in the darkness if they had gone only a few paces further. And their mother told them that it must have been the angel who watches over good children.

Snow-white and Rose-red kept their mother's little cottage so neat that it was a pleasure to look inside it. In the summer Rose-red took care of the house and every morning laid a wreath of flowers by her mother's bed before she awoke, in which was a rose from each tree. In the winter Snow-white lit the fire and hung the kettle on the wrekin. The kettle was of copper and shone like gold, so brightly was it polished. In the evening, when the snow-flakes fell, the mother said, 'Go, Snow-white, and bolt the door,' and then they sat round the hearth, and the mother took her spectacles and read aloud out of a large book, and the two girls listened as they sat and span. And close by them lay a lamb upon the floor, and behind them upon a perch sat a white dove with its head hidden beneath its wings.

One evening, as they were thus sitting comfortably together, someone knocked at the door as if he wished to be let in. The mother said, 'Quick, Rose-red, open the door; it must be a traveller who is seeking shelter.' Rose-red went and pushed back the bolt, thinking that it was a poor man, but it was not; it was a bear that stretched his broad, black head within the door.

Rose-red screamed and sprang back, the lamb bleated, the dove fluttered, and Snow-white hid herself behind her mother's bed. But the bear began to speak and said, 'Do not be afraid, I will do you no harm! I am half-frozen and only want to warm myself a little beside you.'

'Poor bear,' said the mother, 'lie down by the fire, only take care that you do not burn your coat.' Then she cried, 'Snow-white, Rose-red, come out; the bear will do you no harm, he means well.' So they both came out, and by-and-by the lamb and dove came nearer, and were not afraid of him. The bear said, 'Here, children, knock the snow out of my coat a little,' so they brought the broom and swept the bear's hide clean; and he stretched himself by the fire and growled contentedly and comfortably. It was not long before they grew quite at home, and played tricks with their clumsy guest. They tugged his hair with their hands, put their feet upon his back and rolled him about, or they took a hazel-switch and beat him, and when he growled they laughed. But the bear took it all in good part, only when they were too rough he called out, 'Leave me alive, children,

> Snowy-white, Rosy-red,
> Will you beat your lover dead?'

When it was bed-time, and the others went to bed, the mother said to the bear, 'You can lie there by the hearth, and then you will be safe from the cold and the bad weather.' As soon as day dawned the two children let him out, and he trotted across the snow into the forest.

Henceforth the bear came every evening at the same time, laid himself down by the hearth, and let the children amuse themselves with him as much as they liked; and they got so used to him that the doors were never fastened until their black friend had arrived.

When spring had come and all outside was green, the bear said one morning to Snow-white, 'Now I must go away, and cannot come back for the whole summer.'

'Where are you going, then, dear bear?' asked Snow-white.

'I must go into the forest and guard my treasures from the wicked dwarfs. In the winter, when the earth is frozen hard, they are obliged to stay below and cannot work their way through; but now, when the sun has thawed and warmed the earth, they break through it, and come out to pry and steal; and what once gets into their hands and in their caves, does not easily see daylight again.'

Snow-white was quite sorry for his going away, and as she unbolted the door for him, and the bear was hurrying out, he caught against the bolt and a piece of his hairy coat was torn off, and it seemed to Snow-white as if she had seen gold shining through it, but she was not sure about it. The bear ran away quickly and was soon out of sight behind the trees.

A short time afterwards the mother sent her children into the forest to get firewood. There they found a big tree which lay felled on the ground, and close by the trunk something was jumping backwards and forwards in the grass, but they could not make out what it was. When they came nearer they saw a dwarf with an old, withered face and a snow-white beard a yard long. The end of the beard was caught in a crevice of the tree, and the little fellow was jumping backwards and forwards like a dog tied to a rope, and did not know what to do.

He glared at the girls with his fiery, red eyes and cried, 'Why do you stand there? Can you not come here and help me?'

'What are you about there, little man?' asked Rose-red.

'You stupid, prying goose!' answered the dwarf; 'I was going to split the tree to get a little wood for cooking. The little bit of food that one of us wants gets burnt up directly with thick logs; we do not swallow so much as you coarse, greedy folk. I had just driven the wedge safely in, and everything was going as I wished, but the wretched wood was too smooth and suddenly sprang asunder, and the tree closed so quickly that I could not pull out my beautiful white beard; so now it is tight in and I cannot get away, and the silly, sleek, milk-faced things laugh! Ugh! how odious you are!'

The children tried very hard, but they could not pull the beard out, it was caught too fast. 'I will run and fetch someone,' said Rose-red.

'You senseless goose!' snarled the dwarf; 'why should you fetch someone? You are already two too many for me; can you not think of something better?'

'Don't be impatient,' said Snow-white, 'I will help you,' and she pulled her scissors out of her pocket, and cut off the end of the beard.

As soon as the dwarf felt himself free he laid hold of a bag which lay amongst the roots of the tree, and which was full of gold, and lifted it up, grumbling to himself, 'Uncouth people, to cut off a piece of my fine beard. Bad luck to you!' and then he swung the bag upon his back, and went off without even once looking at the children.

Some time after that Snow-white and Rose-red went to catch a dish of fish. As they came near the brook they saw something like a large grasshopper jumping towards the water, as if it were going to leap in. They ran to it and found it was the dwarf.

'Where are you going?' said Rose-red; 'you surely don't want to go into the water?'

'I am not such a fool!' cried the dwarf; 'don't you see that the accursed fish wants to pull me in?' The little man had been sitting there fishing, and unluckily the wind had twisted his beard with the fishing-line; just then a big fish bit, and the feeble creature had not strength to pull it out. The fish kept the upper hand and pulled the dwarf towards him. He held on to all the reeds and rushes, but it was of little good; he was forced to follow the movements of the fish and was in urgent danger of being pulled into the water.

The girls came just in time; they held him fast and tried to free his beard from the line, but all in vain—beard and line were entangled fast together. Nothing was left but to bring out the scissors and cut the beard, whereby a small part of it was lost.

When the dwarf saw that he screamed out, 'Is that civil, you toadstool, to disfigure one's face? Was it not enough to clip off the end of my beard? Now you have cut off the best part of it. I cannot let myself be seen by my people. I wish you had been made to run the soles off your shoes!' Then he took out a sack of pearls which lay in the rushes, and without saying a word more he dragged it away and disappeared behind a stone.

It happened that soon afterwards the mother sent the two girls to the town to buy needles and thread, and laces and ribbons. The road led them across a heath upon which huge pieces of rock lay strewn here and there. Now they noticed a large bird hovering in the air, flying slowly round and round above them; it sank lower and lower, and at last settled near a rock not far off. Directly afterwards they heard a loud, piteous cry. They ran up and saw with horror that the eagle had seized their old acquaintance the dwarf, and was going to carry him off.

The children, full of pity, at once took tight hold of the little man, and pulled against the eagle so long that at last he let his booty go. As soon as the dwarf had recovered from his first fright he cried with his shrill voice, 'Could you not have done it more carefully? You dragged at my brown coat so that it is all torn and full of holes, you helpless, clumsy creatures!' Then he took up a sack of precious stones, and slipped away again under the rock into his hole. The girls, who by this time were used to his thanklessness, went on their way and did their business in the town.

As they crossed the heath again on their way home they surprised the dwarf, who had emptied out his bag of precious stones in a clean spot, and had not thought that anyone would come there so late. The evening sun shone upon the brilliant stones; they glittered and sparkled with all colours so beautifully that the children stood still and looked at them.

'Why do you stand gaping there?' cried the dwarf, and his ashen-grey face became copper-red with rage. He was going on with his bad words when a loud growling was heard, and a black bear came trotting towards them out of the forest. The dwarf sprang up in a fright, but he could not get to his cave, for the bear was already close. Then in the dread of his heart he cried, 'Dear Mr Bear, spare me, I will give you all my treasures; look, the beautiful jewels lying there! Grant me my life. What do you want with such a slender little fellow as I? You would not feel me between your teeth. Come, take these two wicked girls; they are tender morsels for you, fat as young quails; for mercy's sake, eat them!'

The bear took no heed of his words, but gave the wicked creature a single blow with his paw, and he did not move again.

The girls had run away, but the bear called to them, 'Snow-white and Rose-red, do not be afraid; wait, I will come with you.' Then they knew his voice and waited, and when he came up to them suddenly his bearskin fell off, and he stood there a handsome man, clothed all in gold. 'I am a King's son,' he said, 'and I was bewitched by that wicked dwarf, who had stolen my treasures; I have had to run about the forest as a savage bear until I was freed by his death. Now he has got his well-deserved punishment.'

Snow-white was married to him, and Rose-red to his brother, and they divided between them the great treasure which the dwarf had gathered together in his cave. The old mother lived peacefully and happily with her children for many years. She took the two rose-trees with her, and they stood before her window, and every year bore the most beautiful roses, white and red.

THE WATER OF LIFE

There was once a King who was so ill that it was thought impossible his life could be saved. He had three sons, and they were all in great distress on his account, and they went into the castle gardens and wept at the thought that he must die. An old man came up to them and asked the cause of their grief. They told him that their father was dying, and nothing could save him. The old man said, 'There is only one remedy which I know; it is the Water of Life. If he drinks of it he will recover, but it is very difficult to find.'

The eldest son said, 'I will soon find it,' and he went to the sick man to ask permission to go in search of the Water of Life, as that was the only thing to cure him.

'No,' said the King. 'The danger is too great. I would rather die.'

But he persisted so long that at last the King gave his permission.

The Prince thought, 'If I bring this water I shall be the favourite, and I shall inherit the kingdom.'

So he set off, and when he had ridden some distance he came upon a dwarf standing in the road, who cried, 'Whither away so fast?'

'Stupid little fellow,' said the Prince, proudly; 'what business is it of yours?' and rode on.

The little man was very angry, and made an evil vow.

Soon after, the Prince came to a gorge in the mountains, and the further he rode the narrower it became, till he could go no further. His horse could neither go forward nor turn round for him to dismount; so there he sat, jammed in.

The sick King waited a long time for him, but he never came back. Then the second son said, 'Father, let me go and find the Water of Life,' thinking, 'if my brother is dead I shall have the kingdom.'

The King at first refused to let him go, but at last he gave his consent. So the Prince started on the same road as his brother, and met the same dwarf, who stopped him and asked where he was going in such a hurry.

'Little Snippet, what does it matter to you?' he said, and rode away without looking back.

But the dwarf cast a spell over him, and he, too, got into a narrow gorge like his brother, where he could neither go backwards nor forwards.

This is what happens to the haughty.

As the second son also stayed away, the youngest one offered to go and fetch the Water of Life, and at last the King was obliged to let him go.

When he met the dwarf, and he asked him where he was hurrying to, he stopped and said, 'I am searching for the Water of Life, because my father is dying.'

'Do you know where it is to be found?'

'No,' said the Prince.

'As you have spoken pleasantly to me, and not been haughty like your false brothers, I will help you and tell you how to find the Water of Life. It flows from a fountain in the courtyard of an enchanted castle; but you will never get in unless I give you an iron rod and two loaves of bread. With the rod strike three times on the iron gate of the castle, and it will spring open. Inside you will find two lions with wide-open jaws, but if you throw a loaf to each they will be quiet. Then you must make haste to fetch the Water of Life before it strikes twelve, or the gates of the castle will close and you will be shut in.'

The Prince thanked him, took the rod and the loaves, and set off. When he reached the castle all was just as the dwarf had said. At the third knock the gate flew open, and when he had pacified the lions with the loaves, he walked into the castle. In the great hall he found several enchanted Princes, and he took the rings from their fingers. He also took a sword and a loaf, which were lying by them. On passing into the next room he found a beautiful maiden, who rejoiced at his coming. She embraced him, and said that he had saved her, and should have the whole of her kingdom; and if he would come back in a year she would marry him. She also told him where to find the fountain with the enchanted water; but, she said, he must make haste to get out of the castle before the clock struck twelve.

Then he went on, and came to a room where there was a beautiful bed freshly made, and as he was very tired he thought he would take a little rest; so he lay down and fell asleep. When he woke it was striking a quarter to twelve. He sprang up in a fright, ran to the fountain and took some of the water in a cup which was lying near, and then hurried away. The clock struck just as he reached the iron gate, and it banged so quickly that it took off a bit of his heel.

He rejoiced at having got some of the Water of Life, and hastened on his homeward journey. He again passed the dwarf, who said, when he saw the sword and the loaf, 'Those things will be of much service to you. You will be able to strike down whole armies with the sword, and the loaf will never come to an end.'

The Prince did not want to go home without his brothers, and he said, 'Good dwarf, can you not tell me where my brothers are? They went in search of the Water of Life before I did, but they never came back.'

'They are both stuck fast in a narrow mountain gorge. I cast a spell over them because of their pride.'

Then the Prince begged so hard that they might be released that at last the dwarf yielded; but he warned him against them and said, 'Beware of them; they have bad hearts.'

He was delighted to see his brothers when they came back, and told them all that had happened to him; how he had found the Water of Life, and brought a goblet full with him. How he had released a beautiful Princess, who would wait a year for him and then marry him, and he would become a great Prince.

Then they rode away together, and came to a land where famine and war were raging. The King thought he would be utterly ruined, so great was the destitution.

The Prince went to him and gave him the loaf, and with it he fed and satisfied his whole kingdom. The Prince also gave him his sword, and he smote the whole army of his enemies with it, and then he was able to live in peace and quiet. Then the Prince took back his sword and his loaf, and the three brothers rode on. But they had to pass through two more countries where war and famine were raging, and each time the Prince gave his sword and his loaf to the King, and in this way he saved three kingdoms.

After that they took a ship and crossed the sea. During the passage the two elder brothers said to each other, 'Our youngest brother found the Water of Life, and we did not, so our father will give him the kingdom which we ought to have, and he will take away our fortune from us.'

This thought made them very vindictive, and they made up their minds to get rid of him. They waited till he was asleep, and then they emptied the Water of Life from his goblet and took it themselves, and filled up his cup with salt sea water.

As soon as they got home the youngest Prince took his goblet to the King, so that he might drink of the water which was to make him well; but after drinking only a few drops of the sea water he became more ill than ever. As he was bewailing himself, his two elder sons came to him and accused the youngest of trying to poison him, and said that they had the real Water of Life, and gave him some. No sooner had he drunk it than he felt better, and he soon became as strong and well as he had been in his youth.

Then the two went to their youngest brother, and mocked him, saying, 'It was you who found the Water of Life; you had all the trouble, while we have the reward. You should have been wiser, and kept your eyes open; we stole it from you while you were asleep on the ship. When the end of the year comes, one of us will go and bring away the beautiful Princess. But don't dare to betray us. Our father will certainly not believe you, and if you say a single word you will lose your life; your only chance is to keep silence.'

The old King was very angry with his youngest son, thinking that he had tried to take his life. So he had the Court assembled to give judgment upon him, and it was decided that he must be secretly got out of the way.

One day when the Prince was going out hunting, thinking no evil, the King's huntsman was ordered to go with him. Seeing the huntsman look sad, the Prince said to him, 'My good huntsman, what is the matter with you?'

The huntsman answered, 'I can't bear to tell you, and yet I must.'

The Prince said, 'Say it out; whatever it is I will forgive you.'

'Alas!' said the huntsman, 'I am to shoot you dead; it is the King's command.'

The Prince was horror-stricken, and said, 'Dear huntsman, do not kill me; give me my life. Let me have your dress, and you shall have my royal robes.'

The huntsman said, 'I will gladly do so; I could never have shot you.' So they changed clothes, and the huntsman went home, but the Prince wandered away into the forest.

After a time three wagon-loads of gold and precious stones came to the King for his youngest son. They were sent by the Kings who had been saved by the Prince's sword and his miraculous loaf, and who now wished to show their gratitude.

Then the old King thought, 'What if my son really was innocent?' and said to his people, 'If only he were still alive! How sorry I am that I ordered him to be killed.'

'He is still alive,' said the huntsman. 'I could not find it in my heart to carry out your commands,' and he told the King what had taken place.

A load fell from the King's heart on hearing the good news, and he sent out a proclamation to all parts of his kingdom that his son was to come home, where he would be received with great favour.

In the meantime, the Princess had caused a road to be made of pure shining gold leading to her castle, and told her people that whoever came riding straight along it would be the true bridegroom, and they were to admit him. But anyone who came either on one side of the road or the other would not be the right one, and he was not to be let in.

When the year had almost passed, the eldest Prince thought that he would hurry to the Princess, and by giving himself out as her deliverer would gain a wife and a kingdom as well. So he rode away, and when he saw the beautiful golden road he thought it would be a thousand pities to ride upon it; so he turned aside, and rode to the right of it. But when he reached the gate the people told him that he was not the true bridegroom, and he had to go away.

Soon after the second Prince came, and when he saw the golden road he thought it would be a thousand pities for his horse to tread upon it; so he turned aside, and rode up on the left of it. But when he reached the gate he was also told that he was not the true bridegroom, and, like his brother, was turned away.

When the year had quite come to an end, the third Prince came out of the wood to ride to his beloved, and through her to forget all his past sorrows. So on he went, thinking only of her, and wishing to be with her; and he never even saw the golden road. His horse cantered right along the middle of it, and when he reached the gate it was flung open and the Princess received him joyfully, and called him her deliverer, and the lord of her kingdom. Their marriage was celebrated without

delay, and with much rejoicing. When it was over, she told him that his father had called him back and forgiven him. So he went to him and told him everything; how his brothers had deceived him, and how they had forced him to keep silence. The old King wanted to punish them, but they had taken a ship and sailed away over the sea, and they never came back as long as they lived.

THE FOUR SKILFUL BROTHERS

There was once a poor man who had four sons, and when they were grown up, he said to them, 'My dear children, you must now go out into the world, for I have nothing to give you; so set out, and go to some distance and learn a trade, and see how you can make your way.'

So the four brothers took their sticks, bade their father farewell, and went through the town-gate together. When they had travelled about for some time, they came to a cross-way which branched off in four different directions. Then said the eldest, 'Here we must separate, but on this day four years, we will meet each other again at this spot, and in the meantime we will seek our fortunes.'

Then each of them went his way, and the eldest met a man who asked him where he was going, and what he was intending to do.

'I want to learn a trade,' he replied.

Then the other said, 'Come with me, and be a thief.'

'No,' he answered, 'that is no longer regarded as a reputable trade, and the end of it is that one has to swing on the gallows.'

'Oh,' said the man, 'you need not be afraid of the gallows; I will only teach you to get such things as no other man could ever lay hold of, and no one will ever detect you.'

So he allowed himself to be talked into it, and while with the man, became an accomplished thief, and so dexterous that nothing was safe from him if he once desired to have it.

The second brother met a man who put the same question to him—what he wanted to learn in the world.

'I don't know yet,' he replied.

'Then come with me, and be an astronomer; there is nothing better than that, for nothing is hid from you.'

He liked the idea, and became such a skilful astronomer that when he had learnt everything and was about to travel onwards, his master gave him a telescope and said to him, 'With that you can see whatsoever takes place either on earth or in heaven, and nothing can remain concealed from you.'

A huntsman took the third brother into training, and gave him such excellent training in everything which related to huntsmanship, that he became an experienced hunter. When he went away, his master gave him a gun and said, 'It will never fail you; whatsoever you aim at, you are certain to hit.'

The youngest brother also met a man who spoke to him, and enquired what his intentions were. 'Would you not like to be a tailor?' said he.

'Not that I know of,' said the youth, 'sitting doubled up from morning till night, driving the needle and the goose backwards and forwards, is not to my taste.'

'Oh, but you are speaking in ignorance,' answered the man; 'with me you would learn a very different kind of tailoring, which is respectable and proper, and for the most part very honourable.'

So he let himself be persuaded, and went with the man, and learnt his art from the very beginning. When they parted, the man gave the youth a needle and said, 'With this you can sew together whatever is given you, whether it is as soft as an egg or as hard as steel; and it will all become one piece of stuff, so that no seam will be visible.'

When the appointed four years were over, the four brothers arrived at the same time at the cross-roads, embraced and kissed each other, and returned home to their father. 'So now,' said he, quite delighted, 'the wind has blown you back again to me.'

They told him of all that had happened to them, and that each had learnt his own trade. Now they were sitting just in front of the house under a large tree, and the father said, 'I will put you all to the test, and see what you can do.' Then he looked up and said to his second son, 'Between two branches up at the top of this tree, there is a chaffinch's nest; tell me how many eggs there are in it?'

The astronomer took his glass, looked up, and said, 'There are five.'

Then the father said to the eldest, 'Fetch the eggs down without disturbing the bird which is sitting hatching them.'

The skilful thief climbed up and took the five eggs from beneath the bird, which never observed what he was doing and remained quietly sitting where she was, and brought them down to his father. The father took them, and put one of them on each corner of the table, and the fifth in the middle, and said to the huntsman, 'With one shot you shall shoot me the five eggs in two, through the middle.'

The huntsman aimed, and shot the eggs, all five as the father had desired, and that at one shot. He certainly must have had some of the powder for shooting round corners.

'Now it's your turn,' said the father to the fourth son; 'you shall sew the eggs together again, and the young birds that are inside them as well, and you must do it so that they are not hurt by the needle.'

The tailor brought his needle and sewed them as his father wished. When he had done this the thief had to climb up the tree again and carry them to the nest, and put them back under the bird without her being aware of it. The bird sat her full time, and after a few days the young ones crept out.

'Well,' said the old man to his sons, 'I begin to think you are worth more than green clover; you have used your time well, and learnt something good. I can't say which of you deserves the most praise. That will be proved if you have but an early opportunity of using your talents.'

Not long after this there was a great uproar in the country, for the King's daughter was carried off by a dragon. The King was full of trouble about it, both by day and night, and caused it to be proclaimed that whosoever brought her back should have her to wife.

The four brothers said to each other, 'This would be a fine opportunity for us to show what we can do!' and resolved to go forth together and liberate the King's daughter.

'I will soon know where she is,' said the astronomer, and looked through his telescope and said, 'I see her already; she is far away from here on a rock in the sea, and the dragon is beside her watching her.' Then he went to the King, and asked for a ship for himself and his brothers, and sailed with them over the sea until they came to the rock. There the King's daughter was sitting, and the dragon was lying asleep on her lap.

The huntsman said, 'I dare not fire; I should kill the beautiful maiden at the same time.'

'Then I will try my art,' said the thief, and he crept thither and stole her away from under the dragon, so quietly and dexterously that the monster never remarked it, but went on snoring.

Full of joy, they hurried off with her on board ship and steered out into the open sea; but the dragon, who when he awoke had found no Princess there, followed them, and came snorting angrily through the air. Just as he was circling above the ship and was about to descend on it, the huntsman shouldered his gun, and shot him to the heart. The monster fell down dead, but was so large and powerful that his fall shattered the whole ship. Fortunately, however, they laid hold of a couple of planks, and swam about the wide sea.

Then again they were in great peril, but the tailor, who was not idle, took his wondrous needle, and with a few stitches sewed the planks together, and they seated themselves upon them and collected together all the fragments of the vessel. Then he sewed these up so skilfully, that in a very short time the ship was seaworthy, and they could go home again in safety.

When the King once more saw his daughter, there were great rejoicings. He said to the four brothers, 'One of you shall have her to wife, but which of you it is to be you must settle among yourselves.'

Then a warm contest arose among them, for each of them preferred his own claim. The astronomer said, 'If I had not seen the princess, all your arts would have been useless, so she is mine.'

The thief said, 'What would have been the use of your seeing, if I had not got her away from the dragon? So she is mine.'

The huntsman said, 'You and the Princess, and all of you, would have been torn to pieces by the dragon if my ball had not hit him, so she is mine.'

The tailor said, 'And if I, by my art, had not sewn the ship together again, you would all of you have been miserably drowned, so she is mine.'

Then the King uttered this saying: 'Each of you has an equal right, and as all of you cannot have the maiden, none of you shall have her, but I will give to each of you, as a reward, half a kingdom.'

The brothers were pleased with this decision, and said, 'It is better thus than that we should be at variance with each other.' Then each of them received half a kingdom, and they lived with their father in the greatest happiness as long as it pleased God.

FAITHFUL JOHN

There was once on a time an old King who was ill, and thought to himself, 'I am lying on what must be my death-bed.' Then said he, 'Tell Faithful John to come to me.'

Faithful John was his favourite servant, and was so called because he had for his whole life long been so true to him. When, therefore, he came beside the bed, the King said to him, 'Most faithful John, I feel my end approaching and have no anxiety except about my son. He is still of tender age and cannot always know how to guide himself. If you do not promise me to teach him everything that he ought to know, and to be his foster-father, I cannot close my eyes in peace.'

160

Then answered Faithful John, 'I will not forsake him, and will serve him with fidelity, even if it should cost me my life.'

On this, the old King said, 'Now I die in comfort and peace.' Then he added, 'After my death, you shall show him the whole castle: all the chambers, halls and vaults, and all the treasures which lie therein, but the last chamber in the long gallery, in which is the picture of the Princess of the Golden Dwelling, you shall not show. If he sees that picture, he will fall violently in love with her and will drop down in a swoon, and go through great danger for her sake; therefore, you must preserve him from that.' And when Faithful John had once more given his promise to the old King about this, the King said no more, but laid his head on his pillow and died.

When the old King had been carried to his grave, Faithful John told the young King all that he had promised his father on his death-bed, and said, 'This will I assuredly perform, and will be faithful to you as I have been faithful to him, even if it should cost me my life.'

When the mourning was over, Faithful John said to him, 'It is now time that you should see your inheritance. I will show you your father's palace.'

Then he took him about everywhere, up and down, and let him see all the riches and the magnificent apartments; only there was one room which he did not open—that in which hung the dangerous picture. The picture was so placed that when the door was opened you looked straight on it, and it was so admirably painted that it seemed to breathe and live, and there was nothing more charming or more beautiful in the whole world. The young King, however, plainly remarked that Faithful John always walked past this one door, and said, 'Why do you never open this one for me?'

'There is something within it,' he replied, 'which would terrify you.'

But the King answered, 'I have seen all the palace, and I will know what is in this room also,' and he went and tried to break open the door by force.

Then Faithful John held him back, and said, 'I promised your father before his death that you should not see that which is in this chamber; it might bring the greatest misfortune on you and on me.'

'Ah, no,' replied the young King, 'if I do not go in, it will be my certain destruction. I should have no rest day or night until I had seen it with my own eyes. I shall not leave the place now until you have unlocked the door.'

Then Faithful John saw that there was no help for it now, and with a heavy heart and many sighs, sought out the key from the great bunch. When he had opened the door, he went in first, and thought by standing before him he could hide the portrait so that the King should not see it in front of him, but what availed that? The King stood on tip-toe and saw it over his shoulder. And when he saw the portrait of the maiden, which was so magnificent and shone with gold and precious stones, he fell fainting on the ground. Faithful John took him up, carried him to his bed, and sorrowfully thought, 'The misfortune has befallen us, Lord God, what will be the end of it?' Then he strengthened him with wine, until he came to himself again.

The first words the King said were, 'Ah, the beautiful portrait! Whose is it?'

'That is the Princess of the Golden Dwelling,' answered Faithful John.

Then the King continued, 'My love for her is so great that if all the leaves on all the trees were tongues they could not declare it. I will give my life to win her. You are my most Faithful John; you must help me.'

The faithful servant considered within himself for a long time how to set about the matter, for it was difficult to obtain even a sight of the King's daughter. At length he thought of a way, and said to the King, 'Everything which she has about her is of gold—tables, chairs, dishes, glasses, bowls and household furniture. Among your treasures are five tons of gold; let one of the goldsmiths of the kingdom work these up into all manner of vessels and utensils, into all kinds of birds, wild beasts and strange animals, such as may please her, and we will go there with them and try our luck.'

The King ordered all the goldsmiths to be brought to him, and they had to work night and day until at last the most splendid things were prepared. When everything was stowed on board a ship, Faithful John put on the dress of a merchant, and the King was forced to do the same in order to make himself quite unrecognisable. Then they sailed across the sea, and sailed on until they came to the town wherein dwelt the Princess of the Golden Dwelling.

Faithful John bade the King stay behind on the ship and wait for him. 'Perhaps I shall bring the Princess with me,' said he, 'therefore, see that everything is in order; have the golden vessels set out and the whole ship decorated.' Then he gathered together in his apron all kinds of gold things and walked straight to the royal palace. When he entered the courtyard of the palace, a beautiful girl was standing there by the well with two golden buckets in her hand, drawing water with them. And when she was just turning round to carry away the sparkling water she saw the stranger and asked who he was. So he answered, 'I am a merchant,' and opened his apron, and let her look in.

Then she cried, 'Oh, what beautiful things!' and put her pails down and looked at the golden wares one after the other. Then said the girl, 'The princess must see these; she has such great pleasure in golden things that she will buy all you have.' She took him by the hand and led him upstairs, for she was the waiting-maid.

When the King's daughter saw the wares, she was quite delighted, and said, 'They are so beautifully worked that I will buy them all from you.'

But Faithful John said, 'I am only the servant of a rich merchant. The things I have here are not to be compared with those my master has in his ship. They are the most beautiful and valuable things that have ever been made in gold.' She wanted to have everything brought to her there, but he said, 'There are so many of them that it would take a great many days to do that, and so many rooms would be required to exhibit them, that your house is not big enough.'

Then her curiosity and longing were still more excited, until at last she said, 'Conduct me to the ship; I will go there myself and behold the treasures of your master.'

On this Faithful John was quite delighted, and led her to the ship, and when the King saw her, he perceived that her beauty was even greater than the picture represented it to be, and thought no other than that his heart would burst in twain. Then she got into the ship, and the King led her within. Faithful John, however, remained behind with the pilot and ordered the ship to be pushed off, saying, 'Set all sail, till it fly like a bird in air.'

Within, however, the King showed the Princess the golden vessels, every one of them, also the wild beasts and strange animals. Many hours went by whilst she was seeing everything, and in her delight she did not observe that the ship was sailing away. After she had looked at the last, she thanked the merchant and wanted to go home, but when she came to the side of the ship, she saw that it was on the deep sea far from land, and hurrying onwards with all sail set. 'Ah,' cried she in her alarm, 'I am betrayed! I am carried away and have fallen into the power of a merchant—I would die rather!'

The King, however, seized her hand, and said, 'I am not a merchant. I am a King, and of no meaner origin than you are, and if I have carried you away with subtlety, that has come to pass because of my exceeding great love for you. The first time that I looked on your portrait, I fell fainting to the ground.' When the Princess of the Golden Dwelling heard that, she was comforted, and her heart was inclined unto him, so that she willingly consented to be his wife.

It happened, however, while they were sailing onwards over the deep sea, that Faithful John, who was sitting on the fore part of the vessel, making music, saw three ravens in the air, which came flying towards them. On this he stopped playing and listened to what they were saying to each other, for that he well understood. One cried, 'Oh, there he is carrying home the Princess of the Golden Dwelling.'

'Yes,' replied the second, 'but he has not got her yet.'

Said the third, 'But he has got her; she is sitting beside him in the ship.'

Then the first began again, and cried, 'What good will that do him? When they reach land a chestnut horse will leap forward to meet him, and the prince will want to mount it, but if he does that, it will run away with him, and rise up into the air with him, and he will never see his maiden more.'

Spoke the second, 'But is there no escape?'

'Oh, yes, if anyone else gets on it swiftly, and takes out the pistol which must be in its holster, and shoots the horse dead with it, the young King is saved. But who knows that? And whosoever does know it, and tells it to him, will be turned to stone from the toe to the knee.'

Then said the second, 'I know more than that; even if the horse be killed, the young King will still not keep his bride. When they go into the castle together, a wrought bridal garment will be lying there in a dish, and looking as if it were woven of gold and silver; it is, however, nothing but sulphur and pitch, and if he put it on, will burn him to the very bone and marrow.'

Said the third, 'Is there no escape at all?'

'Oh, yes,' replied the second, 'if anyone with gloves on seizes the garment and throws it into the fire and burns it, the young King will be saved. But what avails that? Whosoever knows it and tells it to him, half his body will become stone from the knee to the heart.'

Then said the third, 'I know still more; even if the bridal garment be burnt, the young King will still not have his bride. After the wedding, when the dancing begins and the young Queen is dancing, she will suddenly turn pale and fall down as if dead, and if someone does not lift her up and draw three drops of blood from her right shoulder and spit them out again, she will die. But if any one who knows that were to declare it, he would become stone from the crown of his head to the sole of his foot.'

When the ravens had spoken of this together they flew onwards, and Faithful John had well understood everything, but from that time forth he became quiet and sad, for if he concealed what he had heard from his master, the latter would be unfortunate, and if he discovered it to him, he himself must sacrifice his life. At length, however, he said to himself, 'I will save my master, even if it bring destruction on myself.'

When, therefore, they came to shore, all happened as foretold by the ravens, and a magnificent chestnut horse sprang forward. 'Good,' said the King, 'he shall carry me to my palace,' and was about to mount it when Faithful John got before him, jumped quickly on it, drew the pistol out of the holster, and shot the horse.

Then the other attendants of the King, who after all were not very fond of Faithful John, cried, 'How shameful to kill the beautiful animal that was to have carried the King to his palace!'

But the King said, 'Hold your peace and leave him alone; he is my most faithful John, who knows what may be the good of that!'

They went into the palace, and in the hall there stood a dish, and therein lay the bridal garment looking no otherwise than as if it were made of gold and silver. The young King went towards it and was about to take hold of it, but Faithful John pushed him away, seized it with gloves on, carried it quickly to the fire and burnt it. The other attendants again began to murmur, and said, 'Behold, now he is even burning the King's bridal garment!'

But the young King said, 'Who knows what good he may have done; leave him alone, he is my most faithful John.'

And now the wedding was solemnised. The dance began, and the bride also took part in it; then Faithful John was watchful and looked into her face, and suddenly she turned pale and fell to the ground as if she were dead. On this he ran hastily to her, lifted her up and bore her into a chamber—then he laid her down, and knelt and sucked the three drops of blood from her right shoulder, and spat them out. Immediately she breathed again and recovered herself, but the young King had seen this, and being ignorant why Faithful John had done it, was angry and cried, 'Throw him into a dungeon!'

Next morning Faithful John was condemned and led to the gallows, and when he stood on high and was about to be executed, he said, 'Everyone who has to die is permitted before his end to make one last speech. May I too, claim the right?'

'Yes,' answered the King, 'it shall be granted unto you.'

Then said Faithful John, 'I am unjustly condemned, and have always been true to you,' and related how he had hearkened to the conversation of the ravens when on the sea, and how he had been obliged to do all these things in order to save his master. Then cried the King, 'Oh, my most faithful John. Pardon, pardon—bring him down.'

But as Faithful John had spoken the last word he had fallen down lifeless and become a stone.

Thereupon the King and the Queen suffered great anguish, and the King said, 'Ah, how ill I have requited great fidelity!' and ordered the stone figure to be taken up and placed in his bedroom beside his bed. And as often as he looked on it he wept, and said, 'Ah, if I could bring you to life again, my most faithful John.'

Some time passed and the Queen bore twins, two sons who grew fast and were her delight. Once when the Queen was at church and the two children were sitting playing beside their father, the latter full of grief again looked at the stone figure, sighed and said, 'Ah, if I could but bring you to life again, my most faithful John.'

Then the stone began to speak and said, 'You can bring me to life again if you will use for that purpose what is dearest to you.'

Then cried the King, 'I will give everything I have in the world for you.'

The stone continued, 'If you will cut off the heads of your two children with your own hands, and sprinkle me with their blood, I shall be restored to life.'

The King was terrified when he heard that he himself must kill his dearest children, but he thought of Faithful John's great fidelity, and how he had died for him, drew his sword, and with his own hand cut off the children's heads. And when he had smeared the stone with their blood, life returned to it, and Faithful John stood once more safe and healthy before him. He said to the King, 'Your truth shall not go unrewarded,' and took the heads of the children, put them on again, and rubbed the wounds with their blood, on which they became whole again immediately, and jumped about and went on playing as if nothing had happened.

Then the King was full of joy, and when he saw the Queen coming he hid Faithful John and the two children in a great cupboard. When she entered, he said to her, 'Have you been praying in the church?'

'Yes,' answered she, 'but I have constantly been thinking of Faithful John and what misfortune has befallen him through us.'

Then said he, 'Dear wife, we can give him his life again, but it will cost us our two little sons, whom we must sacrifice.'

The Queen turned pale, and her heart was full of terror, but she said, 'We owe it to him, for his great fidelity.'

Then the King was rejoiced that she thought as he had thought, and went and opened the cupboard, and brought forth Faithful John and the children, and said, 'God be praised, he is delivered, and we have our little sons again also,' and told her how everything had occurred.

Then they dwelt together in much happiness until their death.

HANSEL AND GRETHEL

Close to a large forest there lived a woodcutter with his wife and his two children. The boy was called Hansel and the girl Grethel. They were always very poor and had very little to live on, and at one time, when there was famine in the land, he could no longer procure daily bread.

One night he lay in bed worrying over his troubles, and he sighed and said to his wife: 'What is to become of us? How are we to feed our poor children when we have nothing for ourselves?'

'I'll tell you what, husband,' answered the woman, 'tomorrow morning we will take the children out quite early into the thickest part of the forest. We will light a fire, and give each of them a piece of bread; then we will go to our work and leave them alone. They won't be able to find their way back, and so we shall be rid of them.'

'Nay, wife,' said the man, 'we won't do that. I could never find it in my heart to leave my children alone in the forest; the wild animals would soon tear them to pieces.'

'What a fool you are!' she said. 'Then we must all four die of hunger. You may as well plane the boards for our coffins at once.'

She gave him no peace till he consented. 'But I grieve over the poor children all the same,' said the man.

The two children could not go to sleep for hunger either, and they heard what their stepmother said to their father.

Grethel wept bitterly, and said: 'All is over with us now!'

'Be quiet, Grethel!' said Hansel. 'Don't cry; I will find some way out of it.'

When the old people had gone to sleep, he got up, put on his little coat, opened the door, and slipped out. The moon was shining brightly, and the white pebbles round the house shone like newly-minted coins. Hansel stooped down and put as many into his pockets as they would hold.

Then he went back to Grethel, and said: 'Take comfort, little sister, and go to sleep. God won't forsake us.' And then he went to bed again.

When the day broke, before the sun had risen, the woman came and said, 'Get up, you lazy-bones; we are going into the forest to fetch wood.'

Then she gave them each a piece of bread, and said, 'Here is something for your dinner, but mind you don't eat it before, for you'll get no more.'

Grethel put the bread under her apron, for Hansel had the stones in his pockets. Then they all started for the forest.

When they had gone a little way, Hansel stopped and looked back at the cottage, and he did the same thing again and again.

His father said: 'Hansel, what are you stopping to look back at? Take care, and put your best foot foremost.'

'O Father!' said Hansel, 'I am looking at my white cat; it is sitting on the roof, wanting to say good-bye to me.'

'Little fool! that's no cat, it's the morning sun shining on the chimney.'

But Hansel had not been looking at the cat, he had been dropping a pebble on to the ground each time he stopped. When they reached the middle of the forest, their father said:

'Now, children, pick up some wood. I want to make a fire to warm you.'

Hansel and Grethel gathered the twigs together and soon made a huge pile. Then the pile was lighted, and when it blazed up, the woman said, 'Now lie down by the fire and rest yourselves while we go and cut wood; when we have finished we will come back to fetch you.'

Hansel and Grethel sat by the fire, and when dinner-time came they each ate their little bit of bread, and they thought their father was quite near because they could hear the sound of an axe. It was no axe, however, but a branch which the man had tied to a dead tree, and which blew backwards and forwards against it. They sat there such a long time that they got tired, their eyes began to close, and they were soon fast asleep.

When they woke it was dark night. Grethel began to cry: 'How shall we ever get out of the wood!'

But Hansel comforted her, and said, 'Wait a little till the moon rises, then we will soon find our way.'

When the full moon rose, Hansel took his little sister's hand, and they walked on, guided by the pebbles, which glittered like newly-coined money. They walked the whole night, and at daybreak they found themselves back at their father's cottage.

They knocked at the door, and when the woman opened it and saw Hansel and Grethel, she said, 'You bad children, why did you sleep so long in the wood? We thought you did not mean to come back any more.'

But their father was delighted, for it had gone to his heart to leave them behind alone.

Not long after they were again in great destitution, and the children heard the woman at night in bed say to their father: 'We have eaten up everything. The children must go away; we will take them further into the forest so that they won't be able to find their way back. There is nothing else to be done.'

The man took it much to heart, and said, 'We had better share our last crust with the children.'

But the woman would not listen to a word he said; she only scolded and reproached him. Anyone who once says A must also say B, and as he had given in the first time, he had to do so the second also. The children were again wide awake and heard what was said.

When the old people went to sleep, Hansel again got up, meaning to go out and get some more pebbles, but the woman had locked the door and he couldn't get out. But he consoled his little sister, and said: 'Don't cry, Grethel; go to sleep. God will help us.'

In the early morning the woman made the children get up and gave them each a piece of bread, but it was smaller than the last. On the way to the forest Hansel crumbled it up in his pocket, and stopped every now and then to throw a crumb on to the ground.

'Hansel, what are you stopping to look about you for?' asked his father.

'I am looking at my dove which is sitting on the roof and wants to say good-bye to me,' answered Hansel.

'Little fool!' said the woman, 'that is no dove, it is the morning sun shining on the chimney.'

Nevertheless, Hansel strewed the crumbs from time to time on the ground. The woman led the children far into the forest where they had never been in their lives before. Again they made a big fire, and the woman said:

'Stay where you are, children, and when you are tired you may go to sleep for a while. We are going further on to cut wood, and in the evening when we have finished we will come back and fetch you.'

At dinner-time Grethel shared her bread with Hansel, for he had crumbled his up on the road. Then they went to sleep, and the evening passed, but no one came to fetch the poor children.

It was quite dark when they woke up, and Hansel cheered his little sister, and said:

'Wait a bit, Grethel, till the moon rises, then we can see the bread-crumbs which I scattered to show us the way home.'

When the moon rose they started, but they found no bread-crumbs, for all the thousands of birds in the forest had pecked them up and eaten them.

Hansel said to Grethel: 'We shall soon find the way.'

But they could not find it. They walked the whole night, and all the next day from morning till night, but they could not get out of the wood. They were very hungry, for they had nothing to eat but a few berries which they found. They were so tired that their legs would not carry them any further, and they lay down under a tree and went to sleep.

When they woke in the morning it was the third day since they had left their father's cottage.

They started to walk again, but they only got deeper and deeper into the wood, and if no help came they must perish.

At midday they saw a beautiful snow-white bird sitting on a tree. It sang so beautifully that they stood still to listen to it. When it stopped, it fluttered its wings and flew round them. They followed it till they came to a little cottage, on the roof of which it settled itself.

When they got quite near, they saw that the little house was made of bread, and it was roofed with cake; the windows were transparent sugar.

'This will be something for us,' said Hansel. 'We will have a good meal. I will have a piece of the roof, Grethel, and you can have a bit of the window; it will be nice and sweet.'

Hansel stretched up and broke off a piece of the roof to try what it was like. Grethel went to the window and nibbled at that. A gentle voice called out from within:

'Nibbling, nibbling, like a mouse,
Who's nibbling at my little house?'

The children answered:

'The wind, the wind doth blow
From heaven to earth below,'

and went on eating without disturbing themselves. Hansel, who found the roof very good, broke off a large piece for himself; and Grethel pushed a whole round pane out of the window, and sat down on the ground to enjoy it.

All at once the door opened and an old, old woman, supporting herself on a crutch, came hobbling out. Hansel and Grethel were so frightened that they dropped what they held in their hands.

But the old woman only shook her head and said: 'Ah, dear children, who brought you here? Come in and stay with me; you will come to no harm.'

She took them by the hand and led them into the little house. A nice dinner was set before them, pancakes and sugar, milk, apples and nuts. After this she showed them two little white beds into which they crept, and felt as if they were in heaven.

Although the old woman appeared to be so friendly, she was really a wicked old witch who was on the watch for children, and she had built the bread house on purpose to lure them to her. Whenever she could get a child into her clutches she cooked it and ate it, and considered it a grand feast. Witches have red eyes, and can't see very far, but they have keen scent like animals, and can perceive the approach of human beings.

When Hansel and Grethel came near her, she laughed wickedly to herself, and said scornfully, 'Now I have them; they shan't escape me.'

She got up early in the morning, before the children were awake, and when she saw them sleeping, with their beautiful rosy cheeks, she murmured to herself, 'They will be dainty morsels.'

She seized Hansel with her bony hand and carried him off to a little stable, where she shut him up with a barred door; he might shriek as loud as he liked, she took no notice of him. Then she went to Grethel and shook her till she woke, and cried:

'Get up, little lazy-bones, fetch some water and cook something nice for your brother; he is in the stable, and has to be fattened. When he is nice and fat, I will eat him.'

Grethel began to cry bitterly, but it was no use, she had to obey the witch's orders. The best food was now cooked for poor Hansel, but Grethel only had the shells of crayfish.

The old woman hobbled to the stable every morning, and cried: 'Hansel, put your finger out for me to feel how fat you are.'

Hansel put out a knuckle-bone, and the old woman, whose eyes were dim, could not see and thought it was his finger, and she was much astonished that he did not get fat.

When four weeks had passed, and Hansel still kept thin, she became very impatient and would wait no longer.

'Now then, Grethel,' she cried, 'bustle along and fetch the water. Fat or thin, tomorrow I will kill Hansel and eat him.'

Oh, how his poor little sister grieved! As she carried the water, the tears streamed down her cheeks.

'Dear God, help us!' she cried. 'If only the wild animals in the forest had devoured us, we should, at least, have died together.'

'You may spare your lamentations; they will do you no good,' said the old woman.

Early in the morning Grethel had to go out to fill the kettle with water, and then she had to kindle a fire and hang the kettle over it.

'We will bake first,' said the old witch. 'I have heated the oven and kneaded the dough.' She pushed poor Grethel towards the oven, and said: 'Creep in and see if it is properly heated, and then we will put the bread in.'

She meant, when Grethel had got in, to shut the door and roast her. But Grethel saw her intention, and said, 'I don't know how to get in. How am I to manage it?'

'Stupid goose!' cried the witch. 'The opening is big enough; you can see that I could get into it myself.'

She hobbled up, and stuck her head into the oven. But Grethel gave her a push which sent the witch right in, and then she banged the door and bolted it.

'Oh! oh!' she began to howl horribly. But Grethel ran away and left the wicked witch to perish miserably.

Grethel ran as fast as she could to the stable. She opened the door, and cried: 'Hansel, we are saved. The old witch is dead.'

Hansel sprang out, like a bird out of a cage when the door is set open. How delighted they were! They fell upon each other's necks, and kissed each other, and danced about for joy.

As they had nothing more to fear, they went into the witch's house, and they found chests in every corner full of pearls and precious stones.

'These are better than pebbles,' said Hansel, as he filled his pockets.

Grethel said, 'I must take something home with me too.' And she filled her apron.

'But now we must go,' said Hansel, 'so that we may get out of this enchanted wood.'

Before they had gone very far they came to a great piece of water.

'We can't get across it,' said Hansel; 'I see no stepping-stones and no bridge.'

'And there are no boats either,' answered Grethel. 'But there is a duck swiming; it will help us over if we ask it.' So she cried:

> 'Little duck, that cries quack, quack,
> Here Grethel and here Hansel stand.
> Quickly, take us on your back,
> No path nor bridge is there at hand!'

The duck came swimming towards them, and Hansel got on its back and told his sister to sit on his knee.

'No,' answered Grethel, 'it will be too heavy for the duck; it must take us over one after the other.'

The good creature did this, and when they had got safely over and walked for a while, the wood seemed to grow more and more familiar to them, and at last they saw their father's cottage in the distance. They began to run, and rushed inside, where they threw their arms round their father's neck. The man had not had a single happy moment since he had deserted his children in the wood, and in the meantime his wife was dead.

Grethel shook her apron and scattered the pearls and precious stones all over the floor, and Hansel added handful after handful out of his pockets.

So all their troubles came to an end, and they lived together as happily as possible.

RAPUNZEL

There was once a man and his wife who had long wished in vain for a child, when at last they had reason to hope that Heaven would grant their wish. There was a little window at the back of their house, which overlooked a beautiful garden full of lovely flowers and shrubs. It was, however, surrounded by a high wall, and nobody dared to enter it, because it belonged to a powerful witch who was feared by everybody.

One day the woman, standing at this window and looking into the garden, saw a bed planted with beautiful rampion. It looked so fresh and green that it made her long to eat some of it. This longing increased every day, and as she knew it could never be satisfied, she began to look pale and miserable and to pine away. Then her husband was alarmed, and said: 'What ails you, my dear wife?'

'Alas!' she answered, 'if I cannot get any of the rampion from the garden behind our house to eat, I shall die.'

Her husband, who loved her, thought, 'Before you let your wife die, you must fetch her some of that rampion, cost what it may.' So in the twilight he climbed over the wall into the witch's garden, hastily picked a handful of rampion, and took it back to his wife. She immediately dressed it, and ate it up very eagerly. It was so very, very nice, that the next day her longing for it increased threefold. She could have no peace unless her husband fetched her some more. So in the twilight he set out again; but when he got over the wall he was terrified to see the witch before him.

'How dare you come into my garden like a thief, and steal my rampion?' she said, with angry looks. 'It shall be the worse for you!'

'Alas!' he answered, 'be merciful to me; I am only here from necessity. My wife sees your rampion from the window, and she has such a longing for it, that she would die if she could not get some of it.'

The anger of the witch abated, and she said to him, 'If it is as you say, I will allow you to take away with you as much rampion as you like, but on one condition. You must give me the child which your wife is about to bring into the world. I will care for it like a mother, and all will be well with it.' In his fear the man consented to everything, and when the baby was born, the witch appeared, gave it the name of Rapunzel (rampion), and took it away with her.

Rapunzel was the most beautiful child under the sun. When she was twelve years old, the witch shut her up in a tower which stood in a wood. It had neither staircase nor doors, and only a little window quite high up in the wall. When the witch wanted to enter the tower, she stood at the foot of it and cried:

'Rapunzel, Rapunzel, let down your hair.'

Rapunzel had splendid long hair, as fine as spun gold. As soon as she heard the voice of the witch, she unfastened her plaits and twisted them round a hook by the window. They fell twenty ells downwards, and the witch climbed up by them.

It happened a couple of years later that the King's son rode through the forest and came close to the tower. From thence he heard a song so lovely that he stopped to listen. It was Rapunzel, who in her lonelines made her sweet voice resound to pass away the time. The King's son wanted to join her, and he sought for the door of the tower, but there was none to find.

He rode home, but the song had touched his heart so deeply that he went into the forest every day to listen to it. Once, when he was hidden behind a tree, he saw a witch come to the tower and call out:

'Rapunzel, Rapunzel, let down your hair.'

Then Rapunzel lowered her plaits of hair and the witch climbed up to her.

'If that is the ladder by which one ascends,' he thought, 'I will try my luck myself.' And the next day, when it began to grow dark, he went to the tower and cried:

'Rapunzel, Rapunzel, let down your hair.'

The hair fell down at once, and the King's son climbed up by it.

At first Rapunzel was terrified, for she had never set eyes on a man before, but the King's son talked to her kindly, and told her that his heart had been so deeply touched by her song that he had no peace and he was obliged to see her. Then Rapunzel lost her fear, and when he asked if she would have him for her husband, and she saw that he was young and handsome, she thought, 'He will love me better than old Mother Gothel.' So she said, 'Yes,' and laid her hand in his.

She said, 'I will gladly go with you, but I do not know how I am to get down from this tower. When you come, will you bring a skein of silk with you every time. I will twist it into a ladder, and when it is long enough I will descend by it, and you can take me away with you on your horse.'

She arranged with him that he should come and see her every evening, for the old witch came in the daytime.

The witch discovered nothing, till suddenly Rapunzel said to her, 'Tell me, Mother Gothel, how can it be that you are so much heavier to draw up than the young Prince who will be here before long?'

'Oh, you wicked child, what do you say? I thought I had separated you from all the world, and yet you have deceived me.' In her rage she seized Rapunzel's beautiful hair, twisted it twice round her left hand, snatched up a pair of shears and cut off the plaits, which fell to the ground. She was so merciless that she took poor Rapunzel away into a wilderness, where she forced her to live in the greatest grief and misery.

In the evening of the day on which she had banished Rapunzel, the witch fastened the plaits which she had cut off to the hook by the window, and when the Prince came and called:

'Rapunzel, Rapunzel, let down your hair,'

she lowered the hair. The Prince climbed up, but there he found, not his beloved Rapunzel, but the witch, who looked at him with angry and wicked eyes.

'Ah!' she cried mockingly, 'you have come to fetch your lady-love, but the pretty bird is no longer in her nest; and she can sing no more, for the cat has seized her, and it will scratch your own eyes out too. Rapunzel is lost to you; you will never see her again.'

The Prince was beside himself with grief, and in his despair he sprang out of the window. He was not killed, but his eyes were scratched out by the thorns among which he fell. He wandered about blind in the wood, and had nothing but roots and berries to eat. He did nothing but weep and lament over the loss of his beloved wife Rapunzel. In this way he wandered about for some years, till at last he reached the wilderness where Rapunzel had been living in great poverty with the twins who had been born to her, a boy and a girl.

He heard a voice which seemed very familiar to him, and he went towards it. Rapunzel knew him at once, and fell weeping upon his neck. Two of her tears fell upon his eyes, and they immediately grew quite clear, and he could see as well as ever.

He took her to his kingdom, where he was received with joy, and they lived long and happily together.

THE FROG PRINCE

In the olden times, when wishing was some good, there lived a King whose daughters were all beautiful, but the youngest was so lovely that even the sun, that looked on many things, could not but marvel when he shone upon her face.

Near the King's palace there was a large dark forest, and in the forest, under an old lime-tree, was a well. When the day was very hot the Princess used to go into the forest and sit upon the edge of this cool well; and when she was tired of doing nothing she would play with a golden ball, throwing it up in the air and catching it again, and this was her favourite game. Now on one occasion it so happened that the ball did not fall back into her hand stretched up to catch it, but dropped to the ground and rolled straight into the well. The Princess followed it with her eyes, but it disappeared, for the well was so very deep that it was quite impossible to see the bottom. Then she began to cry bitterly, and nothing would comfort her.

As she was lamenting in this manner, someone called out to her, 'What is the matter, Princess? Your lamentations would move the heart of a stone.'

She looked round towards the spot whence the voice came, and saw a frog stretching its broad, ugly face out of the water.

'Oh, it's you, is it, old splasher? I am crying for my golden ball which has fallen into the water.'

'Be quiet then, and stop crying,' answered the frog. 'I know what to do; but what will you give me if I get you back your plaything?'

'Whatever you like, you dear old frog,' she said, 'my clothes, my pearls and diamonds, or even the golden crown upon my head.'

The frog answered, 'I care not for your clothes, your pearls and diamonds, nor even your golden crown; but if you will be fond of me, and let me be your playmate, sit by you at table, eat out of your plate, drink out of your cup, and sleep in your little bed—if you will promise to do all this, I will go down and fetch your ball.'

'I will promise anything you like to ask, if only you will get me back my ball.'

She thought, 'What is the silly old frog chattering about? He lives in the well, croaking with his mates, and he can't be the companion of a human being.'

As soon as the frog received her promise, he ducked his head under the water and disappeared. After a little while, back he came with the ball in his mouth, and threw it on to the grass beside her.

The Princess was full of joy when she saw her pretty toy again, picked it up, and ran off with it.

'Wait, wait,' cried the frog. 'Take me with you; I can't run as fast as you can.'

But what was the good of his crying 'Croak, croak,' as loud as he could? She did not listen to him, but hurried home, and forgot all about the poor frog; and he had to go back to his well.

The next day, as she was sitting at dinner with the King and all the courtiers, eating out of her golden plate, something came flopping up the stairs, flip, flap, flip, flap. When it reached the top it knocked at the door, and cried, 'Youngest daughter of the King, you must let me in.' She ran to see who it was. When she opened the door and saw the frog she shut it again very quickly and went back to the table, for she was very much frightened.

The King saw that her heart was beating very fast, and he said, 'My child, what is the matter? Is there a giant at the door wanting to take you away?'

'Oh no!' she said, 'it's not a giant, but a hideous frog.'

'What does the frog want with you?'

'Oh, father dear, last night when I was playing by the well in the forest my golden ball fell into the water. And I cried, and the frog got it out for me; and then, because he insisted on it, I promised that he should be my playmate. But I never thought that he would come out of the water; but there he is, and he wants to come in to me.'

He knocked at the door for the second time, and sang:

'Youngest daughter of the King,
Take me up, I sing;
Know'st thou not what yesterday
Thou to me didst say
By the well in forest dell.
Youngest daughter of the King,
Take me up, I sing.'

Then said the King, 'What you have promised you must perform. Go and open the door for him.'

So she opened the door, and the frog shuffled in, keeping close to her feet, till he reached her chair. Then he cried, 'Lift me up beside you.' She hesitated, till the King ordered her to do it. When the frog was put on the chair, he demanded to be placed upon the table, and then he said, 'Push your golden plate nearer that we may eat together.' She did as he asked her, but very unwillingly, as could easily be seen. The frog made a good dinner, but the Princess could not swallow a morsel. At last he said, 'I have eaten enough, and I am tired; carry me into your bedroom and arrange your silken bed, that we may go to sleep.'

The Princess began to cry, for she was afraid of the clammy frog, which she did not dare to touch and which was now to sleep in her pretty little silken bed.

But the King grew very angry, and said, 'You must not despise anyone who has helped you in your need.'

So she seized him with two fingers and carried him upstairs, where she put him in a corner of her room. When she got into bed, he crept up to her and said, 'I am tired, and I want to go to sleep as well as you. Lift me up, or I will tell your father.'

She was very angry, picked him up, and threw him with all her might against the wall, saying, 'You may rest there as well as you can, you hideous frog.' But when he fell to the ground he was no longer a hideous frog, but a handsome Prince with beautiful friendly eyes.

And at her father's wish he became her beloved companion and husband. He told her that he had been bewitched by a wicked fairy, and nobody could have released him from the spells but she herself.

Next morning, when the sun rose, a coach drove up drawn by eight milk-white horses, with white ostrich plumes on their heads, and a golden harness. Behind stood faithful Henry, the Prince's body-servant. The faithful fellow had been so distressed when his master was changed into a frog that he had caused three iron bands to be placed round his heart, lest it should break from grief and pain.

The coach had come to carry the young pair back into the Prince's own kingdom. The faithful Henry helped both of them into the coach and mounted again behind, delighted at his master's deliverance.

They had only gone a little way when the Prince heard a cracking behind him, as if something were breaking. He turned round, and cried:

> 'Henry, the coach is giving way!'
> 'No, Sir, the coach is safe, I say,
> A band from my heart has fall'n in twain,
> For long I suffered woe and pain.
> While you a frog within a well
> Enchanted were by witch's spell!'

Once more he heard the same snapping and cracking, and then again. The Prince thought it must be some part of the carriage breaking, but it was only the bands round faithful Henry's heart which were snapping, because of his great joy at his master's deliverance and happiness.

SNOW-WHITE

It was the middle of winter, and the snowflakes were falling from the sky like feathers. Now, a Queen sat sewing at a window framed in black ebony, and as she sewed she looked out upon the snow. Suddenly she pricked her finger and three drops of blood fell on to the snow. And the red looked so lovely on the white that she thought to herself: 'If only I had a child as white as snow and as red as blood, and as black as the wood of the window frame!' Soon after, she had a daughter, whose hair was black as ebony, while her cheeks were red as blood, and her skin as white as snow; so she was called Snow-white. But when the child was born the Queen died. A year after the King took another wife. She was a handsome woman, but proud and overbearing, and could not endure that anyone should surpass her in beauty. She had a magic looking-glass, and when she stood before it and looked at herself she used to say:

'Mirror, Mirror on the wall,
Who is fairest of us all?'

then the glass answered:

'Queen, thou'rt fairest of them all.'

Then she was content, for she knew that the looking-glass spoke the truth.

But Snow-white grew up and became more and more beautiful, so that when she was seven years old she was as beautiful as the day, and far surpassed the Queen. Once, when the Queen asked her glass:

'Mirror, Mirror on the wall,
Who is fairest of us all?'

it answered:

'Queen, thou art fairest here, I hold,
But Snow-white is fairer a thousandfold.'

Then the Queen was horror-struck, and turned green and yellow with jealousy. From that hour, whenever she saw Snow-white her heart sank, and she hated the little girl.

The pride and envy of her heart grew like a weed, so that she had no rest day nor night. At last she called a huntsman, and said: 'Take the child out into the wood; I will not set eyes on her again. You must kill her and bring me her lungs and liver as tokens.'

The huntsman obeyed, and took Snow-white out into the forest, but when he drew his hunting-knife and was preparing to plunge it into her innocent heart, she began to cry:

'Alas! dear huntsman, spare my life, and I will run away into the wild forest and never come back again.'

And because of her beauty the huntsman had pity on her and said, 'Well, run away, poor child.' Wild beasts will soon devour you, he thought, but still he felt as though a weight were lifted from his heart because he had not been obliged to kill her. And as just at that moment a young fawn came leaping by, he pierced it and took the lungs and liver as tokens to the Queen. The cook was ordered to serve them up in pickle, and the wicked Queen ate them, thinking that they were Snow-white's.

Now the poor child was alone in the great wood, with no living soul near, and she was so frightened that she knew not what to do. Then she began to run, and ran over the sharp stones and through the brambles, while the animals passed her by without harming her. She ran as far as her feet could carry her till it was nearly evening, when she saw a little house and went in to rest. Inside, everything was small, but as neat and clean as could be. A small table covered with a white cloth stood ready with seven small plates, and by every plate was a spoon, knife, fork, and cup. Seven little beds were ranged against the walls covered with snow-white coverlets. As Snow-white was very hungry and thirsty, she ate a little bread and vegetable from each plate, and drank a little wine from each cup, for she did not want to eat up the whole of one portion. Then, being very tired, she lay down in one of the beds. She tried them all but none suited her; one was too short, another too long—all except the seventh, which was just right. She remained in it, said her prayers, and fell asleep.

When it was quite dark the masters of the house came in. They were seven dwarfs, who dug in the mountains for ore. They kindled their lights, and as soon as they could see they noticed that someone had been there, for everything was not in the order in which they had left it.

The first said, 'Who has been sitting in my chair?'
The second said, 'Who has been eating off my plate?'
The third said, 'Who has been nibbling my bread?'
The fourth said, 'Who has been eating my vegetables?'
The fifth said, 'Who has been using my fork?'
The sixth said, 'Who has been cutting with my knife?'
The seventh said, 'Who has been drinking out of my cup?'

Then the first looked and saw a slight impression on his bed, and said, 'Who has been treading on my bed?' The others came running up and said, 'And mine, and mine.' But the seventh, when he looked into his bed, saw Snow-white, who lay there asleep. He called the others, who came up and cried out with astonishment as they held their lights and gazed at Snow-white. 'Heavens! what a beautiful child,' they said, and they were so delighted that they did not wake her up but left her asleep in bed. And the seventh dwarf slept with his comrades, an hour with each, all through the night.

When morning came Snow-white woke up, and when she saw the seven dwarfs she was frightened. But they were very kind, and asked her name.

'I am called Snow-white,' she answered.

'How did you get into our house?' they asked.

Then she told them how her stepmother had wished to get rid of her, how the huntsman had spared her life, and how she had run all day till she had found the house.

Then the dwarfs said, 'Will you look after our household, cook, make the beds, wash, sew and knit, and keep everything neat and clean? If so you shall stay with us and want for nothing.'

'Yes,' said Snow-white, 'with all my heart'; and she stayed with them and kept the house in order.

In the morning they went to the mountain and searched for copper and gold, and in the evening they came back and then their meal had to be ready. All day the maiden was alone, and the good dwarfs warned her and said, 'Beware of your stepmother, who will soon learn that you are here. Don't let anyone in.'

But the Queen, having, as she imagined, eaten Snow-white's liver and lungs, and feeling certain that she was the fairest of all, stepped in front of her glass, and asked:

> 'Mirror, Mirror on the wall,
> Who is fairest of us all?'

The glass answered as usual:

> 'Queen, thou art fairest here, I hold,
> But Snow-white over the fells,
> Who with the seven dwarfs dwells,
> Is fairer still a thousandfold.'

She was dismayed, for she knew that the glass told no lies, and she saw that the hunter had deceived her and that Snow-white still lived. Accordingly she began to wonder afresh how she might compass her death; for as long as she was not the fairest in the land her jealous heart left her no rest. At last she thought of a plan. She dyed her face and dressed up like an old pedlar, so that she was quite unrecognisable. In this guise she crossed over the seven mountains to the home of the seven dwarfs and called out, 'Wares for sale.'

Snow-white peeped out of the window and said, 'Good-day, mother, what have you got to sell?'

'Good wares, fine wares,' she answered, 'laces of every colour.' And she held out one which was made of gay plaited silk.

'I may let the honest woman in,' thought Snow-white, and she unbolted the door and bought the pretty lace.

'Child,' said the old woman, 'what a sight you are; I will lace you properly for once.'

Snow-white made no objection, and placed herself before the old woman to let her lace her with the new lace. But the old woman laced so quickly and tightly that she took away Snow-white's breath and she fell down as though dead.

'Now I am the fairest,' she said to herself, and hurried away.

Not long after the seven dwarfs came home and were horror-struck when they saw their dear little Snow-white lying on the floor without stirring, like one dead. When they saw she was laced too tight they cut the lace, whereupon she began to breathe and soon came back to life again. When the dwarfs heard what had happened, they said that the old pedlar was no other than the wicked Queen. 'Take care not to let anyone in when we are not here,' they said.

Now the wicked Queen, as soon as she got home, went to the glass and asked:

'Mirror, Mirror on the wall,
Who is fairest of us all?'

and it answered as usual:

'Queen, thou art fairest here, I hold,
But Snow-white over the fells,
Who with the seven dwarfs dwells,
Is fairer still a thousandfold.'

When she heard it all her blood flew to her heart, so enraged was she, for she knew that Snow-white had come back to life again. Then she thought to herself, 'I must plan something which will put an end to her.' By means of witchcraft, in which she was skilled, she made a poisoned comb. Next she disguised herself and took the form of a different old woman. She crossed the mountains and came to the home of the seven dwarfs, and knocked at the door calling out, 'Good wares to sell.'

Snow-white looked out of the window and said, 'Go away, I must not let anyone in.'

'At least you may look,' answered the old woman, and she took the poisoned comb and held it up. The child was so pleased with it that she let herself be beguiled, and opened the door.

When she had made a bargain the old woman said, 'Now I will comb your hair properly for once.'

Poor Snow-white, suspecting no evil, let the old woman have her way, but scarcely was the poisoned comb fixed in her hair than the poison took effect and the maiden fell down unconscious.

'You paragon of beauty,' said the wicked woman, 'now it is all over with you,' and she went away.

Happily it was near the time when the seven dwarfs came home. When they saw Snow-white lying on the ground as though dead, they immediately suspected her stepmother, and searched till they found the poisoned comb. No sooner had they removed it than Snow-white came to herself again and related what had happened. They warned her again to be on her guard, and to open the door to no one.

When she got home the Queen stood before her glass and said:

> 'Mirror, Mirror on the wall,
> Who is fairest of us all?'

and it answered as usual:

> 'Queen, thou art fairest here, I hold,
> But Snow-white over the fells,
> Who with the seven dwarfs dwells,
> Is fairer still a thousandfold.'

When she heard the glass speak these words she trembled and quivered with rage.

'Snow-white shall die,' she said, 'even if it cost me my own life.' Thereupon she went into a secret room, which no one ever entered but herself, and made a poisonous apple. Outwardly it was beautiful to look upon, with rosy cheeks, and everyone who saw it longed for it, but whoever ate of it was certain to die. When the apple was ready she dyed her face and dressed herself like an old peasant woman and so crossed the seven hills to the dwarfs' home. There she knocked.

Snow-white put her head out of the window and said, 'I must not let anyone in; the seven dwarfs have forbidden me.'

'It is all the same to me,' said the peasant woman. 'I shall soon get rid of my apples. There, I will give you one.'

'No; I must not take anything.'

'Are you afraid of poison?' said the woman. 'See, I will cut the apple in half; you eat the red side and I will keep the other.'

Now the apple was so cunningly painted that the red half alone was poisoned. Snow-white longed for the apple, and when she saw the peasant woman eating she could hold out no longer, stretched out her hand and took the poisoned half. Scarcely had she put a bit into her mouth than she fell dead to the ground.

The Queen looked with a fiendish glance, and laughed aloud and said, 'White as snow, red as blood, and black as ebony—this time the dwarfs cannot wake you up again.'

And when she got home and asked the looking-glass:

> 'Mirror, Mirror on the wall,
> Who is fairest of us all?'

it answered at last:

> 'Queen, thou'rt fairest of them all.'

Then her jealous heart was at rest—as much at rest as a jealous heart can be. The dwarfs, when they came at evening, found Snow-white lying on the ground, and not a breath escaped her lips; and she was quite dead. They lifted her up and looked to see whether any poison was to be found, unlaced her dress, combed her hair, washed her with wine and water, but it was no use; their dear child was dead. They laid her on a bier, and all seven sat down and bewailed her and lamented over her for three whole days. Then they prepared to bury her, but she looked so fresh and living, and still had such beautiful rosy cheeks, that they said, 'We cannot bury her in the dark earth.' And so they had a transparent glass coffin made, so that she could be seen from every side, laid her inside and wrote on it in letters of gold her name and how she was a King's daughter. Then they set the coffin out on the mountain, and one of them always stayed by and watched it. And the birds came too and mourned for Snow-white, first an owl, then a raven, and lastly a dove.

Now Snow-white lay a long, long time in her coffin, looking as though she were asleep. It happened that a Prince was wandering in the wood, and came to the home of the seven dwarfs to pass the night. He saw the coffin on the mountain and lovely Snow-white inside, and read what was written in golden letters. Then he said to the dwarfs, 'Let me have the coffin; I will give you whatever you like for it.'

But they said, 'We will not give it up for all the gold of the world.'

Then he said, 'Then give it to me as a gift, for I cannot live without Snow-white to gaze upon; and I will honour and reverence it as my dearest treasure.'

When he had said these words the good dwarfs pitied him and gave him the coffin.

The Prince bade his servants carry it on their shoulders. Now it happened that they stumbled over some brushwood, and the shock dislodged the piece of apple from Snow-white's throat. In a short time she opened her eyes, lifted the lid of the coffin, sat up and came back to life again completely.

'Oh, heaven! where am I?' she asked.

The Prince, full of joy, said, 'You are with me,' and he related what had happened, and then said. 'I love you better than all the world; come with me to my father's castle and be my wife.'

Snow-white agreed and went with him, and their wedding was celebrated with great magnificence. Snow-white's wicked stepmother was invited to the feast; and when she had put on her fine clothes she stepped to her glass and asked:

> 'Mirror, Mirror on the wall,
> Who is fairest of us all?'

The glass answered:

> 'Queen, thou art fairest here, I hold
> The young Queen fairer a thousandfold.'

Then the wicked woman uttered a curse, and was so terribly frightened that she didn't know what to do. Yet she had no rest: she felt obliged to go and see the young Queen. And when she came in she recognised Snow-white, and stood stuck still with fear and terror. But iron slippers were heated over the fire, and were soon brought in with tongs and put before her. And she had to step into the red-hot shoes and dance till she fell down dead.

THE SEVEN SWABIANS

Seven Swabians were once together. The first was Master Schulz; the second, Jackli; the third, Marli; the fourth, Jergli; the fifth, Michal; the sixth, Hans; the seventh, Veitli: all seven had made up their minds to travel about the world to seek adventures and perform great deeds. But in order that they might go in security and with arms in their hands, they thought it would be advisable that they should have one solitary, but very strong and very long, spear made for them. This spear all seven of them took in their hands at once; in front walked the boldest and bravest, and that was Master Schulz; all the others followed in a row, and Veitli was the last.

Then it came to pass one day in the haymaking month (July), when they had walked a long distance and still had a long way to go before they reached the village where they were to pass the night, that as they were in a meadow in the twilight a great beetle or hornet flew by them from behind a bush and hummed in a menacing manner. Master Schulz was so terrified that he all but dropped the spear, and a cold perspiration broke out over his whole body. 'Hark! hark!' cried he to his comrades, 'Good heavens! I hear a drum.'

Jackli, who was behind him holding the spear, and who perceived some kind of a smell, said, 'Something is most certainly going on, for I taste powder and matches.'

At these words Master Schulz began to take to flight, and in a trice jumped over a hedge, but as he just happened to jump on to the teeth of a rake which had been left lying there after the haymaking, the handle of it struck against his face and gave him a tremendous blow. 'Oh dear! Oh dear!' screamed Master Schulz. 'Take me prisoner; I surrender! I surrender!'

The other six all leapt over, one on top of the other, crying, 'If you surrender, I surrender too! If you surrender, I surrender too!' At length, as no enemy was there to bind and take them away, they saw that they had been mistaken, and in order that the story might not be known and they be treated as fools and ridiculed, they all swore to each other to hold their peace about it until one of them accidentally spoke of it.

Then they journeyed onwards. The second danger which they survived cannot be compared with the first. Some days afterwards, their path led them through a fallow-field where a hare was sitting sleeping in the sun. Her ears were standing straight up, and her great glassy eyes were wide open. All of them were alarmed at the sight of the horrible wild beast, and they consulted together as to what it would be the least dangerous to do. For if they were to run away, they knew that the

monster would pursue and swallow them whole. So they said, 'We must go through a great and dangerous struggle. Boldly ventured is half won,' and all seven grasped the spear, Master Schulz in front, and Veitli behind. Master Schulz was always trying to keep the spear back, but Veitli had become quite brave while behind, and wanted to dash forward and cried:

'Strike home, in every Swabian's name,
Or else I wish ye may be lame.'

But Hans knew how to meet this, and said:

'Thunder and lightning, it's fine to prate,
But for dragon-hunting thou'rt aye too late.'

Michal cried:

'Nothing is wanting, not even a hair,
Be sure the Devil himself is there.'

Then it was Jergli's turn to speak:

'If it be not, it's at least his mother,
Or else it's the Devil's own step-brother.'

And now Marli had a bright thought, and said to Veitli:

'Advance, Veitli, advance, advance,
And I behind will hold the lance.'

Veitli, however, did not attend to that, and Jackli said:

' 'Tis Schulz's place the first to be,
No one deserves the honour but he.'

Then Master Schulz plucked up his courage, and said gravely:

'Then let us boldly advance to the fight,
And thus we shall show our valour and might.'

Hereupon they all together set on the dragon. Master Schulz crossed himself and prayed for God's assistance, but as all this was of no avail, and he was getting nearer and nearer to the enemy, he screamed, 'Oho! Oho! ho! ho! ho!' in the greatest anguish. This awakened the hare, which in great alarm darted swiftly away. When Master Schulz thus saw her flying from the field of battle, he cried in his joy:

'Quick, Veitli, quick, look there, look there,
The monster's nothing but a hare.'

But the Swabian allies went in search of further adventures, and came to the Moselle, a mossy, quiet, deep river, over which there are few bridges and which in many places people have to cross in boats. As the seven Swabians did not know this, they called to a man who was working on the opposite side of the river, to know how people contrived to get across. The distance and their way of speaking made the man unable to understand what they wanted, and he said, 'What? what?' in the way people speak in the neighbourhood of Trêves. Master Schulz thought he was saying, 'Wade, wade through the water,' and as he was the first, began to set out and went into the Moselle. It was not long before he sank in the mud, and the deep waves which drove against him, but his hat was blown on the opposite shore by the wind, and a frog sat down beside it and croaked, 'Wat, wat, wat.' The other six on the opposite side heard that, and said, 'Oho, comrades, Master Schulz is calling us; if he can wade across, why cannot we?' So they all jumped into the water together in a great hurry and were drowned, and thus one frog took the lives of six of them, and not one of the Swabian allies ever reached home again.

CLEVER GRETHEL

There was once a cook called Grethel, who wore shoes with red rosettes; and when she went out in them, she turned and twisted about gaily, and thought, 'How fine I am!'

After her walk she would take a draught of wine in her light-heartedness; and as wine gives an appetite, she would then taste some of the dishes that she was cooking, saying to herself, 'The cook is bound to know how the food tastes.'

It so happened that one day her master said to her, 'Grethel, I have a guest coming tonight; roast me two fowls in your best style.'

'It shall be done, sir!' answered Grethel. So she killed the chickens, scalded and plucked them, and then put them on the spit; towards evening she put them down to the fire to roast. They got brown and crisp, but still the guest did not come. Then Grethel called to her master, 'If the guest does not come I must take the fowls from the fire; but it will be a thousand pities if they are not eaten soon while they are juicy.'

Her master said, 'I will go and hasten the guest myself.'

Hardly had her master turned his back before Grethel laid the spit with the fowls on it on one side, and said to herself, 'It's thirsty work standing over the fire so long. Who knows when he will come. I'll go down into the cellar in the meantime and take a drop of wine.'

She ran down and held a jug to the tap, then said, 'Here's to your health, Grethel,' and took a good pull. 'Drinking leads to drinking,' she said, 'and it's not easy to give it up,' and again she took a good pull. Then she went upstairs and put the fowls to the fire again, poured some butter over them, and turned the spit round with a will. It smelt so good that she thought, 'There may be something wanting; I must have a taste.' And she passed her finger over the fowls and put it in her mouth. 'Ah, how good they are; it's a sin and a shame that there's nobody to eat them.' She ran to the window to see if her master was coming with the guest, but she saw nobody. Then she went back to the fowls again, and thought, 'One wing is catching a little, better to eat it—and eat it I will.' So she cut it off and ate it with much enjoyment. When it was finished, she thought, 'The other must follow, or the master will notice that something is wanting.' When the wings were consumed she went back to the window again to look for her master, but no one was in sight.

'Who knows,' she thought. 'I dare say they won't come at all; they must have dropped in somewhere else.' Then she said to herself, 'Now, Grethel, don't be afraid, eat it all up; why should good food be wasted? When it's all gone you can rest; run and have another drink and then finish it up.' So she went down to the cellar, took a good drink, and contentedly ate up the rest of the fowl. When it had all disappeared and still no master came, Grethel looked at the other fowl and said, 'Where one is gone the other must follow. What is good for one is right for the other. If I have a drink first I shall be none the worse.' So she took another hearty pull at the jug, and then she sent the other fowl after the first one.

In the height of her enjoyment, her master came back, and cried, 'Hurry, Grethel, the guest is just coming.'

'Very well, sir, I'll soon have it ready,' answered Grethel.

Her master went to see if the table was properly laid, and took the big carving-knife with which he meant to cut up the fowls, to sharpen it. It the meantime the guest came and knocked politely at the door. Grethel ran to see who was there, and, seeing the guest, she put her finger to her lips and said, 'Be quiet, and get away quickly; if my master catches you it will be the worse for you. He certainly invited you to supper, but only with the intention of cutting off both your ears. You can hear him sharpening his knife now.'

The guest heard the knife being sharpened, and hurried off down the steps as fast as he could.

Grethel ran with great agility to her master, shrieking, 'A fine guest you have invited, indeed!'

'Why, what's the matter, Grethel? What do you mean?'

'Well,' she said, 'he has taken the two fowls that I had just put upon the dish, and run off with them.'

'That's a clever trick!' said her master, regretting his fine fowls. 'If he had only left me one so that I had something to eat.'

He called out to him to stop, but the guest pretended not to hear. Then he ran after him, still holding the carving-knife, and cried, 'Only one, only one!'— meaning that the guest should leave him one fowl; but the guest only thought that he meant he was to give him one ear, and he ran as if he were pursued by fire, and so took both his ears safely home.

THE THREE SPINNERS

There was once a girl who was lazy and would not spin, and let her mother say what she would, she could not bring her to it. At last the mother was once so overcome with anger and impatience that she beat her, at which the girl began to weep loud.

Now at this very moment the Queen drove by, and when she heard the weeping she stopped her carriage, went into the house and asked the mother why she was beating her daughter so that the cries could be heard out on the road?

Then the woman was ashamed to reveal the laziness of her daughter, and said, 'I cannot get her to leave off spinning. She insists on spinning for ever and ever, and I am poor, and cannot procure the flax.'

Then the Queen answered, 'There is nothing that I like better to hear than the sound of spinning, and I am never happier than when the wheels are humming. Let me have your daughter with me in the palace; I have flax enough, and there she shall spin as much as she likes.'

The mother was heartily satisfied with this, and the Queen took the girl with her. When they had arrived at the palace, she led her up into three rooms which were filled from the bottom to the top with the finest flax. 'Now spin me this flax,' said she, 'and when you have done it, you shall have my eldest son for a husband, even if you are poor. I care not for that; your indefatigable industry is dowry enough.'

The girl was secretly terrified, for she could not have spun the flax, no, not if she had lived till she was three hundred years old, and had sat at it every day from morning till night. When, therefore, she was alone, she began to weep, and sat thus for three days without moving a finger.

On the third day came the Queen, and when she saw that nothing had been spun yet, she was surprised; but the girl excused herself by saying that she had not been able to begin because of her great distress at leaving her mother's house. The Queen was satisfied with this, but said, when she was going away, 'Tomorrow you must begin to work.'

When the girl was alone again, she did not know what to do, and in her distress went to the window. Then she saw three women coming towards her, the first of whom had a broad flat foot, the second, such a great underlip that it hung down over her chin, and the third, a broad thumb. They remained standing before the window, and asked the girl what was amiss with her? She complained of her trouble, and then they offered her their help and said, 'If you will invite us to the wedding, not be ashamed of us, and will call us your aunts, and also will place us at your table, we will spin up the flax for you, and that in a very short time.'

'With all my heart,' she replied. 'Do but come in and begin the work at once.'

Then she let in the three strange women, and they seated themselves and began their spinning. The one drew the thread and trod the wheel, the other wetted the thread, the third twisted it, and struck the table with her finger, and as often as she struck it, a skein of thread fell to the ground that was spun in the finest manner possible. The girl concealed the three spinners from the Queen, and showed her whenever she came the great quantity of spun thread, until the latter could not praise her enough. When the first room was empty she went to the second, and at last to the third, and that too was quickly cleared. Then the three women took leave, and said to the girl, 'Do not forget what you have promised us; it will make your fortune.'

When the maiden showed the Queen the empty rooms and the great heap of yarn, she gave orders for the wedding, and the bridegroom rejoiced that he was to have such a clever and industrious wife, and praised her mightily. 'I have three aunts,' said the girl, 'and as they have been very kind to me, I should not like to forget them in my good fortune; allow me to invite them to the wedding, and let them sit with us at table.'

The Queen and the bridegroom said, 'Why should we not allow that?'

Therefore, when the feast began, the three women entered in strange apparel, and the bride said, 'Welcome, dear aunts.'

'Ah,' said the bridegroom, 'how do you come by such ugly friends?'

Thereupon he went to the one with the broad flat foot, and said, 'How do you come by such a broad foot?'

'By treading,' she answered.

Then the bridegroom went to the second, and said, 'How do you come by your falling lip?'

'By licking,' she answered.

Then he asked the third, 'How do you come by your broad thumb?'

'By twisting the thread,' she answered.

On this the King's son was alarmed and said, 'Neither now nor ever shall my beautiful bride touch a spinning-wheel.'

And thus she got rid of the hateful flax-spinning.

CLEVER ELSA

There was once a man who had a daughter called Clever Elsa. When she was grown-up, her father said: 'We must get her married.'

'Yes,' said her mother; 'if only somebody came who would have her.'

At last a suitor, named Hans, came from a distance. He made an offer for her on condition that she really was as clever as she was said to be.

'Oh!' said her father, 'she is a long-headed lass.'

And her mother said: 'She can see the wind blowing in the street and hear the flies coughing.'

'Well,' said Hans, 'if she is not really clever, I won't have her.'

When they were at dinner, her mother said: 'Elsa, go to the cellar and draw some beer.'

Clever Elsa took the jug from the nail on the wall, and went to the cellar, clattering the lid as she went, to pass the time. When she reached the cellar she placed a chair near the cask so that she need not hurt her back by stooping. Then she put down the jug before her and turned the tap. And while the beer was running, so as not to be idle, she let her eyes rove all over the place, looking this way and that.

Suddenly she discovered, just above her head, a pickaxe which a mason had by chance left hanging among the rafters.

Clever Elsa burst into tears, and said: 'If I marry Hans, and we have a child, when it grows big and we send it down to draw beer, the pickaxe will fall on its head and kill it.' So there she sat crying and lamenting loudly at the impending mishap.

The others sat upstairs waiting for the beer, but Clever Elsa never came back. Then the mistress said to her servant: 'Go down to the cellar and see why Elsa does not come back.'

The maid went, and found Elsa sitting by the cask, weeping bitterly. 'Why, Elsa, whatever are you crying for?' she asked.

'Alas!' she answered, 'have I not cause to cry? If I marry Hans, and we have a child, when it grows big, and we send it down to draw beer, perhaps the pickaxe will fall on its head and kill it.'

Then the maid said: 'What a Clever Elsa we have!' and she sat down by Elsa and began to cry over the misfortune.

After a time, as the maid did not come back, and they were growing very thirsty, the master said to the serving-man: 'Go down to the cellar and see what has become of Elsa and the maid.'

The man went down, and there sat Elsa and the maid weeping together. So he said: 'What are you crying for?'

'Alas!' said Elsa, 'have I not enough to cry for? If I marry Hans, and we have a child, and we send it when it is big enough into the cellar to draw beer, the pickaxe will fall on its head and kill it.'

The man said: 'What a clever Elsa we have!' and he, too, joined them and howled in company.

The people upstairs waited a long time for the serving-man, but as he did not come back, the husband said to his wife: 'Go down to the cellar yourself, and see what has become of Elsa.'

So the mistress went down and found all three making loud lamentations, and she asked the cause of their grief. Then Elsa told her that her future child would be killed by the falling of the pickaxe when it was big enough to be sent to draw the beer. Her mother said with the others: 'Did you ever see such a Clever Elsa as we have?'

Her husband upstairs waited some time, but as his wife did not return, and his thirst grew greater, he said: 'I must go to the cellar myself to see what has become of Elsa.'

But when he got to the cellar, and found all the others sitting together in tears, caused by the fear that the child which Elsa might one day have, if she married Hans, might be killed, when it went to draw beer, by the falling of the pickaxe, he too cried: 'What a Clever Elsa we have!'

Then he, too, sat down and added his lamentations to theirs.

The bridegroom waited alone upstairs for a long time; then, as nobody came back, he thought: 'They must be waiting for me down there; I must go and see what they are doing.'

So down he went, and when he found them all crying and lamenting in a heart-broken manner, each one louder than the other, he asked: 'What misfortune can possibly have happened?'

'Alas, dear Hans!' said Elsa, 'if we marry and have a child, and we send it to draw beer when it is big enough, it may be killed if that pickaxe left hanging there were to fall on its head. Have we not cause to lament?'

'Well,' said Hans, 'more wits than this I do not need; and as you are such a Clever Elsa I will have your for my wife.'

He took her by the hand, led her upstairs, and they celebrated the marriage.

When they had been married for a while, Hans said: 'Wife, I am going to work to earn some money; do you go into the fields and cut the corn, so that we may have some bread.'

'Yes, my dear Hans; I will go at once.'

When Hans had gone out, she made some good broth and took it into the field with her.

When she got there, she said to herself: 'What shall I do, reap first, or eat first? I will eat first.'

So she finished up the bowl of broth, which she found very satisfying, so she said again: 'Which shall I do, sleep first, or reap first? I will sleep first.' So she lay down among the corn and went to sleep.

Hans had been home a long time, and no Elsa came, so he said: 'What a Clever Elsa I have. She is so industrious, she does not even come home to eat.'

But as she still did not come, and it was getting dusk, Hans went out to see how much corn she had cut. He found that she had not cut any at all, and that she was lying there fast asleep. Hans hurried home to fetch a fowler's net with little bells on it, and this he hung around her without waking her. Then he ran home, shut the house door, and sat down to work.

At last, when it was quite dark, Clever Elsa woke up, and when she got up there was such a jangling, and the bells jingled at every step she took. She was terribly frightened, and wondered whether she really was Clever Elsa or not, and said: 'Is it me, or is it not me?'

But she did not know what to answer, and stood for a time doubtful. At last she thought: 'I will go home, and ask if it is me, or if it is not me; they will be sure to know.'

She ran to the house, but found the door locked; so she knocked at the window, and cried: 'Hans, is Elsa at home?'

'Yes,' answered Hans, 'she is!'

Then she started and cried: 'Alas! then it is not me,' and she went to another door; but when the people heard the jingling of the bells, they would not open the door, and nowhere would they take her in.

So she ran away out of the village, and was never seen again.